Happy Holiday
Jennifer Faye

a lighthouse café christmas

Bluestar Island, Book 3

Jennifer Faye

Lazy Dazy Press

Copyright © 2021 by **Jennifer F. Stroka**

All rights reserved. No part of this publication may be reproduced, distributed or transmitted in any form or by any means, without prior written permission.

Jennifer Faye/Lazy Dazy Press
P.O. Box 1736
Greensburg, PA 15601
www.JenniferFaye.com

Publisher's Note: This is a work of fiction. Names, characters, places, and incidents are a product of the author's imagination. Locales and public names are sometimes used for atmospheric purposes. Any resemblance to actual people, living or dead, or to businesses, companies, events, institutions, or locales is completely coincidental.

Book Layout © 2017 BookDesignTemplates.com

A Lighthouse Café Christmas: A Second Chance Small Town Romance/ Jennifer Faye. -- 1st ed.
ISBN 978-1-942680-18-5

To Writer Kitty...
Thank you for helping me write this book and all of the others before it by keeping my butt in the chair and my hands on the keyboard. Your little pawprints are forever tattooed upon my heart.

Bluestar Island series:

Book 1: Love Blooms
Book 2: Harvest Dance
Book 3: A Lighthouse Café Christmas
Book 4: Rising Star

Thanks & much appreciation to:
Content Editor: Trenda London
Copy Editor: Lia Fairchild

ABOUT THIS BOOK

As Bluestar Island prepares for a very special Christmas wedding, Santa's sleigh crashes into The Lighthouse Café, reuniting Bluestar's beloved waitress with her former fiancé.

In this holiday novella, Darla Evans has carved out a quiet life for herself as a waitress at The Lighthouse Café. Up until this point, she's conveniently avoided the one man who shattered her heart and her dreams. But when a wedding draws him back to the island, she knows their meetup is unavoidable.

Tech entrepreneur William "Will" Campbell has returned to his childhood home to be the best man in his father's wedding. But first his father has a very special task for him—to restore a sleigh in time for the wedding. However, there's not much time until Christmas. He just might need some help.

As snowflakes cover the small town of Bluestar, Will and Darla work together to make it a very special holiday wedding. With the past looming between them, will the magic of the season open their hearts and allow them to find love again?

Includes a holiday recipe for Darla's frosted sugar cookies!

contents

Chapter One 10
Chapter Two 17
Chapter Three 23
Chapter Four 30
Chapter Five 39
Chapter Six 45
Chapter Seven 51
Chapter Eight 57
Chapter Nine 70
Chapter Ten 77
Chapter Eleven 84
Chapter Twelve 96
Chapter Thirteen 107
Chapter Fourteen 111
Chapter Fifteen 120
Chapter Sixteen 129
Chapter Seventeen 135
Chapter Eighteen 143
Chapter Nineteen 154
Chapter Twenty 162
Epilogue 172
Darla's Frosted Sugar Cookies Recipe 178
Word from Jennifer Faye 180
Other titles by Jennifer Faye 181
About Author 182

1

16 days until Christmas

"Jingle Bells" played on the speakers. Darla Evans mouthed the words. Her steps were light and quick. The holidays were upon them. It was her absolute favorite time of the year. And this year was going better than others. Her college roommate, Aster, had moved to the island. And Darla was hoping for a promotion to assistant manager of The Lighthouse Café.

She'd been waiting tables at Bluestar's most popular restaurant off and on since she was a teenager. She never thought she'd be working there thirteen years later. Life never seemed to work out the way she'd planned, but it didn't stop her from dreaming.

A smile pulled at her lips. It could be Christmas every day of the year, and she'd be happy with it. What could be better than colorful decorations, twinkle lights, and a friendly smile on most everyone's face?

Except for Agnes Dewey. Her smile was more like a

frown. But she didn't count, because she was Bluestar's honorary Scrooge. Darla felt sorry for the woman. She'd always wondered what had put Agnes in a permanently grouchy mood. Some people thought she'd been jilted by a man when she was young. Others thought Agnes had been born with a frown on her face.

Either way, Darla wasn't going to let the woman's sour disposition ruin her good mood. It was a little more than two weeks until Christmas, and she had already finished her Christmas shopping. She'd gotten a new purse for her mother—one that her mother had been oohing and aahing over at Sew Delightful Boutique. For her father, she'd gotten a new fishing rod that he refused to buy himself because his old one would "do for a few more years."

And for her cousin, the mayor, she'd gotten a blue tie with little lighthouses on it. She didn't know if he'd wear it, but she couldn't resist it when she'd seen it at a men's store on the mainland. For her best friend, Aster, she'd gotten a cookbook because now that she and Sam were engaged, Aster was trying hard to improve her domestic skills in between her work at city hall.

And that was pretty much Darla's shopping list. Of course, she'd gotten little gifts for her other friends. This year she'd gotten each of them a lighthouse ornament and chocolate.

A ding of the bell meant her order was up...Agnes's order of a hot turkey sandwich and mashed potatoes smothered in gravy. Darla moved swiftly to the counter. If Agnes thought her food had waited so much as a minute, she would send it back to the kitchen, claiming it

was cold. Darla resisted rolling her eyes. Sometimes she thought Agnes complained just so she'd have something to talk about.

Darla grabbed the warm plate and moved to Agnes's table. She briefly noticed the café didn't have a lot of holiday vibe, with its beachy blue walls decorated with ocean murals. Still, there was a Christmas tree on the long counter at the back of the restaurant. The spacious dining room was filled with small wooden tables made of whitewash wood. Each had a lighthouse ornament on the table that lit up. It wasn't a lot of holiday spirit, but she supposed something was more than nothing.

On her way to Agnes's table, two couples waved goodnight and headed for the door. It was a quiet Thursday evening, and she was the only server working. In fact, she'd been left in charge this evening—something that was happening with more frequency in the last couple of months.

Darla placed the oval plate in front of her. "Can I get you anything else?"

"Yes. I need another fork. There's a mark on this one." She held out the offending utensil.

"Certainly." As Darla walked away with the fork, she didn't notice anything wrong with it other than a little water mark. But she knew Agnes wasn't happy unless she found something wrong with her meal, and so she grabbed another fork from behind the counter, gave it a visual inspection, and then took it to Agnes. "Here you go. Is there anything else?"

"I was reading your horoscope today, and it predicted

this would be a day of great change."

Darla wasn't sure what surprised her more, that Agnes seemed to remember everyone's birthday or that she recalled everyone's horoscope. "And how's your day been?"

Agnes shrugged. "Pretty much the same as always. Too many tourists for the holidays. Too much noise. Too much holiday cheer."

"But surely you have to enjoy something about the holidays, right?" She really hoped the woman found it in her heart to enjoy Christmas.

"Bah…too much is made of it." She inspected her new fork before plunging it into the mashed potatoes.

Darla took that as her cue to move on. A big change was coming. She doubted it. It was already almost six o'clock in the evening. If a big change was coming, shouldn't it have been there already?

She shoved aside the prediction. She had other matters on her mind. Like the upcoming Christmas Eve wedding of Helen Bell and Chief Walter Campbell. She was so happy for them, but she also knew the wedding would mean that Will would be coming to the island. And she wasn't ready to see him. In fact, if she never saw him again, it'd be all right with her.

In the seven years since they'd called off their wedding, she'd been able to avoid him. Since he rarely visited the island, she was able to arrange to be on the mainland when he was there. She either spent some time in Boston or she went on vacation. But this time was different. This time she wasn't able to take the time off from the café. Besides, she was expected to attend the wedding.

Maybe enough time had passed, and she'd feel absolutely nothing when she looked at him. Maybe it was time to leave it all in the past. Could it really be that simple?

As she stood behind the counter, Darla stared out the window. Evening had settled in early. In the glow of the lampposts, she saw a light snow had started. Was that the change Agnes had predicted?

As soon as the thought came to her, she dismissed it. Sure, Agnes's predictions often came true, but that didn't mean the woman was right all of the time. Besides, a big change could mean anything. Her predictions were always just vague enough to mean just about anything.

While Agnes ate her meal, Darla cleared the surrounding tables. As the Christmas carols played on the local radio station, she hummed along. When the tables were cleaned and reset, she moved on to refilling the salt and pepper shakers. She loved quiet evenings like this. It gave her a chance to brainstorm the next scene in her book—or in this case, the opening of a new book—a sequel to the book where she'd just typed her two favorite words: *The End.*

The little bell above the door jingled. Darla glanced up to find Agnes leaving without so much as a "goodnight" or "have a good evening" or at the very least a "thank you." She sighed. Some things never changed.

This was it. The last table for the evening. The kitchen crew was already cleaning the grill and washing the dishes. Darla just needed to clear, clean, and reset this last table.

She stacked the dirty dishes and then wiped down the tabletop. When she went to wipe off the seat, she found Agnes's purse. *Oh no.* Agnes would be in a panic when she realized it was missing. She grabbed it and headed for the door.

She ran out the door. "Agnes!"

Through the snow she saw the woman across the street. She wasn't that far away. If she hurried, she could catch her. She moved through the snow as quickly as she dared.

"Agnes! Agnes, wait up!"

The woman paused and turned. "Darla, what's wrong?"

Darla came to a stop next to Agnes. She held up the purse. "You forgot this."

The woman's mouth gaped. "So I did." She reached for it. "Well, um, thank you. I wouldn't have forgotten it if it wasn't for all of that loud Christmas music and you singing." Agnes turned and continued along the sidewalk.

Darla sighed. At least Agnes thanked her before she was blamed for Agnes's forgetfulness. Darla turned and walked away. The kitchen crew was waiting on her so they could finish cleaning up. And going home early meant more time to write. That thought spurred her steps to come faster. She stepped off the curb and headed across the street.

Honk! Honk!

She looked to her left and was blinded by headlights.

Her heart leapt into her throat. She slipped on the icy asphalt. Her hands and knees took the brunt of the fall. And yet the truck kept coming. Closer. And closer.

2

What had started as a dusting of snow had morphed into large flakes.

William "Will" Campbell didn't smile. This unpredictable winter weather was making everything more difficult. At least he remembered how to drive under these conditions: slow and steady.

He'd just flown from his home in San Francisco to the East Coast that morning. His father, Fire Chief Walter Campbell, had picked him up at Boston Logan International Airport. There was no point in Will renting a car, seeing as cars weren't permitted on the island—at least not without a good excuse and a day pass.

His father had been in a great mood, happier than he'd seen him in years. And he had good reason to be— his father was getting married. Will had returned to the island to be his father's best man. He was happy for his father to have found love again. He didn't think his father would ever move on after Will's mother had died more than nineteen years ago. It was a long time to be alone.

But to see his father with Helen Bell, you could see the happiness on his face and hear it in his voice. The man looked at least ten years younger. Even his steps were lighter and not quite as fast. He was no longer racing toward something because he'd already found what he wanted: love and happiness.

Will wished he could say the same thing about himself. When he'd finished high school and started college, he'd thought he had life all figured out. He knew what he wanted—a stellar career in the tech industry. And though he'd reached heights only few could achieve, it wasn't the complete fulfillment he thought it would be. There was still something missing.

But he didn't have time to worry about that at the moment. Will had returned to the island a couple of weeks ahead of the Christmas Eve wedding because he'd needed to speak to his father. In fact the conversation had been long overdue.

So, while they had been on the mainland, Will told his father that he had been sick. The kind of sick that isn't fixed with a hot bowl of chicken soup and a couple of painkillers. His father had been shocked, worried, and then relieved that Will was now in remission. It was a lot for his father to absorb, but Will didn't want to linger on his health issues. There was an upcoming wedding that needed their attention.

His father wanted to surprise his bride with a horse-drawn sleigh to whisk them away from the church. Will didn't see the need for so much fuss. What was wrong with a decorated golf cart? It'd be a lot simpler. But his father wouldn't hear of it.

However, there was a catch. *Wasn't there always?* The sleigh was old and it hadn't been used in years. In order for it to be ready for the wedding, it needed to be worked on. That was where Will came in. The plan was to move the sleigh from the Evans's small garage over to his father's two-bay garage, which had been all cleared out for the sleigh.

Lucky for him the sleigh had wheels or at least he'd thought he was lucky until they went to roll the sleigh onto the trailer. The wheels didn't want to turn. Everything was rusted and needed lubrication. Trying to get the sleigh ready in time for the wedding felt like it was going to be a full-time job.

It had taken Mr. Evans, Greg Hoover, Will's father, and himself to get the sleigh loaded onto the trailer. It had been quite a job too. At least they could leave it on the trailer until they got all of the wheels working smoothly.

He just had to sneak it through town because his father lived on the other side of town from the Evans's. And it was too late in the day to get a day pass, and he didn't want to wait. He needed to start the restoration work right away. He'd just zip across town with a pickup that his father had borrowed from Sam Bell—Will's future stepbrother. How hard could this be?

As he made his way through Bluestar, a few people did a doubletake when they saw him coming down the road in Sam's pickup. They hesitated and then waved. He waved back. He hoped they didn't notice the lack of a bright orange permit in the window and call the sheriff on him.

Finding Atlantic Drive too congested with golf carts, he zigzagged through town and ended up on Main Street—the road his father lived on. As he crawled down the road, he turned up the windshield wipers. When he tapped the brakes, he noticed the roads were growing slick. And Bluestar's limited road maintenance crew hadn't been out yet.

He was almost to The Lighthouse Café. He knew from his father that Darling, erm, Darla had been working there ever since she'd moved back to the island.

And then the familiar black wooden sign came into sight. A spotlight mounted to the lighthouse-shaped building highlighted the sign. He smiled as he took in the painted image of a red and white lighthouse and the name, *The Lighthouse Café*, scrolled out in white paint. Boy had he missed frequenting it.

Every time he passed by the café, he was tempted to step inside. In fact, he had eaten at the café but Darla was never around when he was in town visiting his father. He had a feeling it was intentional. She hadn't forgiven him for upending their wedding plans.

A movement in the corner of his eye caught his attention. Someone darted out in the road. His breath hitched.

He pressed on the brakes. With the road growing slick, the truck didn't slow down. His chest tightened.

He laid on the horn. It blew loud and long. The woman slipped. She fell right in the roadway.

He stomped both feet on the brake pedal. He willed the truck to stop. The tires finally caught on the pavement. The old pickup and the trailer shuttered to a halt.

He climbed out of the pickup and rushed forward. "Are you all right?"

The woman lifted her chin and her wide-eyed stare met his. "I'm fine."

"Darling." The endearing name he'd been calling her since high school came rushing out. He held his hand out to her. "Let me help you up."

Her gaze turned dark. She didn't accept his hand as she stood on her own. "It's Darla. And I've got it."

"Are you sure you're all right?"

She frowned at him before brushing the snow from her waitress uniform. "I'm fine. What are you doing here?"

"I'm in town for my father's wedding."

"No. What are you doing here with that?" She gestured to the pickup.

"I'm moving something for my father. Not many people are out in the snow, and I thought I could slip through town unnoticed."

She arched a fine brow. "Unnoticed in Bluestar? Really?"

He shrugged. "Okay. You have a point. But I just needed to get this over with and city hall wasn't open, so I was hoping to fly under the radar."

"You don't even have a day pass."

He shrugged. "What can I say? I'm still impatient."

"Why doesn't that surprise me?" She continued to frown. "I have to go."

"I'll be seeing you." A smile tugged at his lips. The thought of seeing Darling, erm, Darla again made him happy. It was past time they fixed things between them.

He stood on the quiet roadway lit by the streetlamps and watched as Darling made her way into the café. It certainly wasn't the reunion he'd hoped for. Wait. Was he hoping to see her again?

With a shake of his head, he climbed back into the pickup. He put the truck in gear and pressed the accelerator, but the pickup didn't go anywhere. The tires spun. *Just great. What else can go wrong?*

He put the pickup in Reverse and pressed lightly on the gas. This section of town sat on a slight grade so going backward wouldn't take much effort. Once the pickup was out of the tire tracks that had turned to ice, he pressed on the accelerator. The truck hesitated. He pressed harder. The pickup leapt forward. He was once more on his way.

He glanced in the rearview mirror to find the trailer rolling in the wrong direction. *What?*

He stomped the brakes. But there was no time to react. Everything was already in motion. The trailer jumped the curb. It was headed for The Lighthouse Café.

3

arling? Really?

Darla refused to give in to the desire to glance over her shoulder—to drink in the handsome features of Will's face. How was it possible that he'd grown better looking during their time apart?

The least he could have done was to lose his thick hair that made her fingers tingle with the desire to run them through it. Or lost his trim body and put on some weight, but he hadn't done any of those things. If anything he might be a bit thinner, as though he worked out daily.

As she made her way back inside the café, she fumed over the fact that her ex not only came close to running her down, but he was also calling her by the pet name he'd bestowed upon her back in high school. *How dare he?*

So much for thinking they could act like calm, rational adults around each other. She didn't know how she'd do it, but she would somehow avoid Will for the remainder of his visit—even if it meant missing the

wedding. The thought weighed heavy on her because she'd known Chief Campbell and Helen Bell her entire life. But if that was what it took to avoid Will, then she'd do it.

Crash!

The sound of shattering glass sent Darla's heart into her throat. The breath suspended in her lungs. She swung around to look in the direction of the ruckus. She blinked, not quite believing her eyes.

Because what she saw was Santa's sleigh. It had crashed through the large picture window in the front of the café. Luckily, no one was seated there.

How had Santa's sleigh ended up in the café? Well, it wasn't quite the entire sleigh, it was the backend. As she got closer, she noticed the tarp had been partially torn off in the collision. She came to a stop a few feet from the sleigh. She recognized it as belonging to her family. It had been handed down through the family for generations. Her parents normally stored it in their garage. So how in the world had it ended up here?

She rushed out the door. She expected to see her father standing outside. But she didn't see him anywhere. There was the loose trailer with the sleigh on top of it. It had jumped the curb and came to a stop against the wall of the café but not before the back part of the trailer and the sleigh had crashed through the big plate glass window. *Oh, what a mess!*

Pete Willoughby, the owner of the café, had gone home early, leaving her in charge. She didn't want to call him and tell him this. It hadn't been that long since the café had been damaged in a big storm before the Harvest Dance that had wreaked damage all over the island. And now this...

Not to mention that this incident could put her promotion to assistant manager in jeopardy. What was Pete going to say? After all, it wasn't like she'd been driving the sleigh.

As the shock wore off, she realized who was behind this entire mess. Will.

Before she phoned Pete, she needed to get to the bottom of how exactly this accident had happened. Why would Will be driving through town at this hour with Santa's sleigh in tow? When she'd spoken to her mother that morning, she hadn't mentioned anything about it. They'd discussed getting together for dinner soon, but there hadn't been any mention of the sleigh. She would have remembered it. Darla had loved that sleigh since she was a kid. She was a big reason why her parents had retained ownership of it, even though it hadn't been used in a number of years.

She hurried outside and found Will rushing toward her. "What happened?"

His eyes widened. "Darling, I'm sorry."

She couldn't remember the last time he'd called her by her proper name. At first, his name for her had been endearing and then it had become the norm. But after so much time had passed and how painfully they'd ended things, it felt like a slap in the face.

"I'm not your darling." Her voice was firm and her gaze steady.

His gaze momentarily widened as though he hadn't

noticed the blunder until she'd pointed it out. "Oh. Right." His gaze moved to the sleigh. "How are the people in the café?"

"Fine. I mean there's no one in the dining room." Her gaze moved to the broken window. "How did this happen?"

"I didn't even know the trailer had pulled loose until I glanced in the rearview mirror. I'm really sorry."

Her gaze moved between him and the sleigh as she tried to make sense of this. "What are you doing with my sleigh?"

His dark brows rose. "Your sleigh?"

Why did he have to pick now to be specific? "My family's sleigh. What are you doing with it?"

"I was taking it to my father's place because his garage is bigger."

She still didn't understand. "Why are you moving it?"

"Oh. You don't know?"

She pressed her hands to her hips as she frowned at him. "Obviously not or I wouldn't be asking you."

"Let me get this moved and then I'll answer your questions." Will moved to the back of the pickup.

She glanced around to find a small crowd had started to form. It wouldn't take long for the news to reach Pete.

"This isn't good." Will vocalized her thoughts.

"Don't tell me it gets worse." She approached the back of the truck. "What's the matter besides the obvious?"

"It's the hitch on the back of the truck. It snapped."

"What does that mean?"

"That I can't move the trailer. Not until I locate another vehicle with a secure hitch."

"And how long is that going to take?"

He raked his fingers through his thick dark hair. "I don't know."

"But the sleigh can't stay here."

"Don't you think I know that?" He pulled out his phone.

She had her own phone call to make, and it wasn't going to be a pleasant one. Pete wasn't going to believe her. After all, it wasn't every day that Santa's sleigh wrecked into the café.

Perhaps proof would help. She withdrew her phone from her pocket. She snapped a picture. She noticed how the entire window was shattered. And snow was starting to get inside the restaurant. It was going to need to be boarded up for the night.

She needed to show some initiative if she were to be promoted. She pulled up Ethan Walker's number. Since moving to the island last spring, he'd quickly become Bluestar's Fix-It-Man. If it was broken, Ethan could usually handle it. He answered the phone on the second ring. When she explained that Santa had run into the café, he burst out laughing. He thought it was some sort of holiday joke, until she told him it was most definitely not a joke. Then he said he had some plywood and would be over to board up the window.

Next she had to call Pete before someone else told him what had happened. She selected his number from her list of contacts. The phone rang once, twice… She

was starting to wonder if it was possible to just leave him a voicemail. But her luck ran out after the fourth ring.

"Evans, this better be important. I was just about to beat my kids at Monopoly."

"Well, sir, I wanted you to know that I have everything under control." Her gaze moved to the trailer and sleigh that were still pressed up against the café. "It's all being taken care of."

"What's being taken care of?" Concern rang out in his voice. "Do I need to come down there?"

"Sir, you don't have to ruin your evening. I can handle this."

"You still haven't told me the problem. Is there a fire?"

"No, sir. Nothing that serious. It's Santa's sleigh. It kind of ran into the café."

"What?" Disbelief rang out in his voice. "You're telling me Santa ran into the café?"

"Yes, sir. I mean, no sir. It's just the sleigh. It was being towed but the hitch broke, and it rolled back into the restaurant. One window is broken."

"Broken?"

"Yes. But don't worry. No one is hurt."

"I need to see this for myself. I'm on my way." The line went dead.

So much for her being in charge. This was going to ruin her chance of filling the upcoming assistant manager vacancy. And the one person she had to blame for this stroke of bad luck was Will.

She turned to him. "What are you doing?"

He was hunched down, working on the backend of the pickup. He had a ratchet in his hand. "I'm trying to remove this bolt."

He attached the ratchet and pushed with all his might to the point where his face turned red from effort. The bolt didn't give way. Not at all. He paused, took up a new position in order to put his entire body behind the effort and then he pushed on the handle. Still nothing.

"This hitch is completely rusted. I'm not going to be able to budge it."

Her gaze moved back to the sleigh, which was taking on a fresh layer of snow. "It can't just stay here."

"Don't worry. I called a friend. He'll be here shortly to tow it away. But then there's the window—"

"Ethan Walker is coming over to board it up."

He smiled at her. "It seems like after all of this time that we still make a good team."

She didn't know what he expected her to say to his proclamation. After all, he was the one who had ended things. He was the one who said they had no future. To her that meant they didn't make a good team.

4

Talk about a string of bad luck.

Will busied himself, trying to remove the broken hitch, but with all of the rust, it wasn't budging, not one little bit. Thankfully, Darling, erm, Darla wasn't quite so stubborn. She'd given up shooting daggers at him with her beautiful eyes and moved back inside the café.

Up until this point, she'd made a point of avoiding him. She'd never given him a chance to apologize—not taking his phone calls right after their breakup and going so far as being off the island any time he visited his father. He could only imagine how much she hated him. He wished he could change her feelings toward him, but he'd resigned himself to the fact that it wasn't going to happen.

His gaze moved to the broken window of The Lighthouse Café. Inside, Darla stood with her back to him. He couldn't help but wonder if that was intentional. Was it wrong that he'd hoped with the years that had passed that things would have somehow healed between them?

The sound of a vehicle approaching drew him from his thoughts. Will turned to find a familiar red pickup pulling to a stop. Oh, boy, he hoped the sheriff didn't catch them. Because neither of their vehicles had a day pass. And he didn't think the sheriff would be impressed with his story about the urgent necessity to move the sleigh across town.

Ethan Walker climbed out of the pickup with Hannah Bell by his side. "Hey, Will, when did you get back to the island?"

"I flew in this morning." Will raked his fingers through his hair. "Dad got this great idea about surprising Helen with a sleigh ride after the wedding, but he didn't realize the sleigh hadn't been used in a number of years so it's not in the best condition. I was moving it to Dad's garage when, uh, someone ran out in front of the pickup. I slammed the brakes, which must have been enough to break the rusty hitch. And well you can see what happened."

Both Ethan and Hannah moved past him to have a look at the damage. "Yikes," Ethan said. "Pete isn't going to be happy about this."

"Tell me about it. It's a good thing I like the enchiladas at Katrina's Kantina because I don't know if he'll let me in the café after this."

"It's not that bad," Hannah offered with a weak smile.

It was bad. She knew it, though she was too kind to say it. And he knew it. Things like this didn't happen in

Bluestar.

"What's going on here?"

The deep, authoritative voice had Will inwardly groaning. This evening was going from awful to downright miserable. He knew without turning around that the sheriff was standing right behind him. And he didn't have to look to know that the sheriff already had his pen and book in hand to write him a ticket with a hefty fine. Bluestar didn't go light with penalties for breaking the no-vehicle rule. It kept people from doing what he'd just done. It was a good thing he could afford the stiff penalty as well as Ethan's ticket. Because Ethan wouldn't be there if it weren't for him.

Will straightened his shoulders and turned. "Hey, sheriff. Sorry about this."

"What exactly is going on? And why is Santa's sleigh crashed into The Lighthouse Café?"

"See. That's a funny story." As the sheriff frowned at him, Will understood that he didn't find any part of this amusing.

This was going to be a long night. A very long night.

He was back early. Much too early.

Darla hadn't been prepared to see Will again—not tonight—not with him looking so utterly handsome. She inwardly groaned as Pete stood in the snow, overseeing the placement of the plywood over the broken window. His hands were pressed to his sides as his clean-shaven face frowned.

Santa's sleigh crashing into the café was going to be

the talk of the town this holiday season and perhaps many future ones. On the upside, maybe the town's gossips would be too busy to talk about Will and her. Could she be that lucky?

But then again, what was there to talk about? Their breakup was old news. And it wasn't like they were going to see much of each other while he was home. Because she intended to keep her distance.

Her gaze moved toward the sleigh as a growing group of men worked to remove it without causing more damage to the café and the sleigh. The antique sleigh had been around her whole life. After her grandfather had passed on, she'd begged her parents to keep it. She remembered being young and excited when Santa would arrive with a red sack full of toys. She'd been too young to know it was her grandfather all dressed up, but she could remember the feeling of wonder and the little bit of magic. She wanted the children of Bluestar to feel that again but her spare time was consumed by her writing. She just hadn't had time to work on the sleigh. And she wondered if it was too late for that dream.

She got busy cleaning up as much of the broken glass as she could until the sleigh was moved. With that task concluded, she moved behind the counter to make some hot chocolate for the group of people standing in the snow. She knew they were trying to decide how best to move the sleigh.

By the time she placed the last cap on the to-go cups and headed for the door, the sleigh was moved out of the window. She rushed outside, pleased to find the snow had lightened. She handed out the hot chocolate to a group of eight men.

When she neared Will, she heard him say, "I'm really sorry about this, Pete. I'll make sure it gets repaired."

Pete wasn't as tall as Will, but he was just as wide in the shoulders. Her boss glanced at the chipped paint from the trim and the shattered window before turning back to Will. "Don't worry about it. That's what insurance is for. Just concentrate on fixing the sleigh."

"Are you sure?" There was a hesitant note in Will's voice.

"Yeah. I needed to replace the windows anyway." Pete glanced toward the sleigh that had just been hitched to Ethan's truck. "How bad is the sleigh?"

"It's not good."

Silently, Darla held the hot chocolate out to Will. When his gaze met hers, she saw the worry reflected in his eyes. Exactly how bad was the sleigh?

She didn't have long to contemplate the answer to the question because as soon as he reached for the cup, their fingers touched, and a jolt of awareness sparked her nerve endings.

Her heart beat a rapid *pitter-patter*. And the breath became lodged in her throat. She should say something, anything. And yet she couldn't think of a word. Her brain and her mouth were at a complete disconnect. It had been so long since they'd been together, and yet her body reacted to him as though no time had passed at all. Her body instinctively leaned toward him as though to lean into his embrace and press her lips to his.

Thankfully, she caught herself before making a scene.

She halted her out-of-control thoughts. Certain Will had a firm hold on the cup, she jerked her hand back. The physical disconnect seemed to help.

Her brain could once again function. "What is the damage to the sleigh?"

He stepped back to let her pass. "Have a look for yourself."

She moved to the other side of the trailer. The gray tarp had been pulled back, and she could see the back corner of the sleigh had been pushed in. The old green paint had cracked and was pulling away from the body. It wasn't good. And she hated that she'd played a part in the accident. If only she hadn't been in such a rush and stepped out into the roadway without looking, none of this would have happened.

She turned to Will. "But I don't understand. What are you doing with the sleigh?"

Will glanced around as though making sure no one overheard him. "It's for the wedding."

"What does this have to do with your father's wedding?"

"Shh...we don't want everyone to know."

She lowered her voice. "Isn't it a little late for that? I'm pretty certain by morning every person on the island is going to know about the accident."

He pursed his lips together. "You're right. For a second I forgot how efficient the gossip mill is in Bluestar. I guess this means we'll need a cover story."

"We?" She wasn't so sure she wanted to be caught up in anything that had to do with her ex.

He nodded. "We need to explain the sleigh being here."

"Why can't you just tell them that you were moving it for the wedding?" It seemed simple enough to her.

"Because my father wants to surprise Helen on their wedding day. I'm moving it to his garage where I'm supposed to spiff it up. It needs a fresh coat of paint, and it would appear the wheels need lubricated as they aren't working very well."

"It has been a lot of years since it's been used." Her parents had never taken it out of storage. "But I wonder why my mother didn't mention this to me."

"It was all last minute. My father didn't think he'd be able to pull it off until he found out I could come back to the island early."

Her gaze moved back to the damage. "There's no way you'll have it repaired in time for the wedding. I feel so bad. If I hadn't run out into the road, chasing after Agnes Dewey—"

"Why were you chasing her?"

"Because she forgot her purse. I just wish this"—she gestured to the sleigh again—"was more easily resolved."

Will tilted his head to the side, like he did every time he was in deep thought. "Maybe it can be."

"I'm not following."

"I can't get all of this work done on my own, but if you were to help me, we could get twice as much work done in half the time."

Surely she hadn't heard him correctly. Had he really

just suggested they work together?

She shook her head. "I don't think it's a good idea."

His gaze challenged her. "Are you really going to let what happened between us ruin our chance to make the perfect Christmas wedding for the happy couple?"

She opened her mouth but then wordlessly closed it. What was she to do? She couldn't forget about her part in the debacle, but to be fair, vehicles weren't normally driven through Bluestar. But if she had paused and looked both ways, would this all have been avoided? Probably.

"I don't know anything about repairing sleighs," she said.

"Do you know how to paint?" When she nodded, he asked, "And can you work a sewing machine?"

"A sewing machine?" How was that going to help fix the sleigh?

He nodded. "The cushions in the sleigh are old and splitting. They need replaced."

She resisted the urge to glance inside the sleigh to make sure what he was saying was correct. It appeared the sleigh needed a lot more help than she'd originally thought. "Yes, I can work a sewing machine."

"Good. Then you're hired. Meet me at my father's garage tomorrow morning."

She stared at him for a few long seconds. Was he serious? When he didn't smile or laugh, she knew he was perfectly serious. They were going to work on the sleigh together.

The thought of spending time with her ex did not thrill her. There had to be a way around it. Maybe they could work on the sleigh at different times. Yes, that sounded reasonable. And it wasn't like she was going to haul her mother's sewing machine out to the garage to make new cushions. No, those she could do at her parents' house. Suddenly, this was seeming a little less stressful and a little more doable.

"I'll see you in the morning." He turned and walked away.

She couldn't believe she'd agreed to work with Will, of all people. But if he thought this meant everything between them was forgotten, he had another thing coming.

5

15 days until Christmas

This was his chance to fix things.

It was an opportunity he never thought he'd get. But was it possible to repair the damage after all of this time?

The following morning, after a trip to city hall to pay the traffic tickets, Will entered his father's garage. He let out a long yawn. He'd been up most of the night, researching how to fix the dented corner. But that was only part of the reason he'd been awake a large portion of the night.

The other reason sleep had alluded him was that he hadn't been prepared to see Dar—la. Sure, he knew they would eventually run into each other, but he didn't expect it to be his first day on the island.

And then there was that moment when their hands had touched. It was like time had been suspended. His heart had slammed into his chest. What had that been about? They'd broken up years ago. There was no way there was anything between them.

He hadn't wanted to see her again to rekindle anything. He wanted to apologize to her for how poorly he'd handled their breakup. He'd never gotten the opportunity. It had bothered him all of this time.

He told himself that once he did—once he made things right between them—he'd be able to move on. Because he didn't want to be single the rest of his life. Sure, he'd dated since Darla, but none of those relationships had turned into anything serious. He blamed it on himself—on the guilt he carried around for hurting Darla.

"I'm here."

The sound of Darla's voice drew him from his thoughts. "Good morning." He gestured to the to-go cup of coffee sitting on the workbench. "I was out today so I picked up coffee for both of us."

Her gaze moved to the coffee. "Skim and two sweeteners."

"Yes. Just the way you like it." The fact he still remembered the way she preferred her coffee didn't go unnoticed by him.

Her face softened with a smile. "Thank you."

While she retrieved the coffee and savored it with a sound that loosely resembled a purr, he struggled not to smile. It'd been so long since he'd heard that sound, and he'd forgotten how much he enjoyed hearing it.

"I did some research on the repairs," he said. "And it appears there's a few ways to go about it."

She walked over to peer at the smushed-in corner, leaving a respectable distance between them. "I wish I had something to add to this conversation, but I've got nothing for you. Sorry."

"It's okay. I just need a sounding board at this point." And so, he went through all of the options he'd been able to come up with from a suction pull, which wouldn't work since this was on a corner, to hammering it out.

"The metal is old and rusty," she said. "Whatever you do, you'll have to be really careful."

He rubbed the back of his neck. "Do you think there are any Santa sleigh repair shops?"

Darla smiled at his question. A real smile that puffed up her cheeks and made her eyes twinkle. "Maybe if you try the North Pole."

"That's not a bad idea." He wasn't ready to let go of this light and fun moment. He reached for his phone in his back pocket. He pulled up the screen. "Should I search for the North Pole sleigh repair shop?"

She continued to smile and shake her head. "You haven't changed."

"Changed?" He wasn't sure what she was referring to.

She nodded. "You always find a way to lighten things when they get too serious." The smile faded from her face as though a memory from their past had come back to her. "But we don't have time to joke around. The wedding will be here before we're ready."

"You're right. How about we split up the duties?"

She sent him a hesitant look. "Such as?"

"Well…" He had an idea of how things should work,

but he wasn't sure if Darla would see it his way. Maybe he should get her input. "What do you have in mind?"

A pleased look filtered over her beautiful face. She strolled around the sleigh, taking time to look inside at the peeling paint and the tattered cushions. And then she even bent over to inspect the underside.

He'd already done all of this, so he stood back and let her do her thing. He couldn't help but wonder if she would want to do things the same as him. That was one of their problems when they'd been engaged—they could never agree on things. He'd want to go out to eat, and she'd want to do take-out at home. He'd want to lie on the couch and watch football on Sundays, while she'd want to go to the park. He supposed that was part of what led him to putting the brakes on their pending marriage. A small part.

He still remembered the day he'd called things off. It had been the second worst day in his life—the worst being the day his mother died. Nothing could compare with that staggering loss for an eleven-year-old or watching how her illness had drained the life out of his father. Still, breaking up with Darla came in a close second.

Darla pressed her hands to her waist. "It doesn't look too bad."

Was she looking at the same sleigh as him? He blinked. Yep, it still looked bad. "I don't know if it's even worth working on."

"What?" She swung around and frowned at him. "How can you say that? Of course, it's worth working on."

He rubbed the back of his neck. "Have you seen the amount of rust? It starts on the runners and carries over to the body. Too bad they didn't have fiberglass or plastic when they made this."

"So, you're giving up?" She leveled her shoulders. "It seems to me that whenever things get too difficult that you quit. Why should this be any different?"

Ouch! Her comment pierced a tender spot in his chest—a place he thought was immune from the hurt of the past. Less than twenty-four hours together and Darla had already pulled the scabs off the past.

But she was wrong about him being a quitter. He wasn't. He was a realist. There was a difference. "It's not like that—"

"We're not having this discussion." She shook her head. "This was a mistake. I never should have agreed to work with you."

And with that she turned and stormed out of the garage.

Is that what she really thought? That he'd ended their engagement because life had become too difficult? That he hadn't been willing to fight to make things work between them?

But how did you fight for something you knew wasn't right for either of them? They'd started walking in two different directions. She kept talking about what they would do when they moved back to the island while he was busy setting the plans in motion to start his own business on the west coast. It was another issue but not the final one.

When he realized the direction of his thoughts, he halted them. He wasn't going there. The past was best left in the past. He needed to be focused on the here and now.

6

14 days until Christmas

What came next?

Who should say what?

The following afternoon, Darla sat on her couch with her laptop resting on her legs. Those were the questions she preferred to concentrate on instead of the other thoughts Will had evoked in her. Had he ended things between them because he hadn't been willing to do the hard work to keep them together? Or had there been something more, or rather, someone else? These questions had tortured her for a long time.

They'd been friends as kids and then became a couple in high school. When you were close to someone for that long, well, there were things you took for granted. Like she'd always assumed Will would be next to her through the thick and thin. It was something she never doubted. But after moving to San Francisco, things had slowly changed.

He'd graduated from college early and started

working long hours. He'd been too tired to talk much when he was home. And so, she'd turned to writing fiction to deal with her loneliness. She hadn't talked to him about her stories, because she had been too insecure to share her writing. It was precious to her—so important that she couldn't risk having someone laugh at it or point out that it was boring. Was that where their troubles had begun? Or had it started before that?

Darla leaned back against the couch and sighed. She should be working on the sleigh today. She'd let her emotions and insecurities get the best of her yesterday. She regretted it.

She couldn't keep avoiding Will. This was an awfully small island. They needed to figure out how to co-exist. But she wasn't ready to face him so soon. And tomorrow she had to work all day. Perhaps come Monday she'd give the arrangement another go.

Knock-knock.

Darla blinked and found her laptop had gone into sleep mode because it had been so long since she'd written a word. She was working on the second book in a series—a series she hadn't tried to sell—a series she kept hidden from the world.

Knock-knock.

She wasn't expecting anyone that afternoon. She'd lucked out that week and gotten all day Saturday off from The Lighthouse Café. Was it Will? Her heart beat faster. She quickly dismissed the idea as she closed her laptop and set it aside. He didn't know where she lived—not that it would be hard for him to find out her address.

But why would he seek her out? They were working together for a good cause, nothing more.

She moved to the door and peered through the peephole to find her bestie on the other side. Darla swung the door open. "Aster, what are you doing here?"

"I came to see you. Now that I've moved into my own apartment, I feel like I never see you anymore."

A gust of cold air rushed past Darla. Goosebumps trailed up her arms. "Come in out of the cold."

Once inside, Aster slipped off her coat and laid it over the back of one of Darla's mismatched chairs. "So, how's it going?"

"Good." She wasn't exactly sure what Aster was referring to.

Aster frowned at her. "Now tell me the truth. What's it like seeing Will again?"

Darla shrugged. What was she supposed to say? That he could still make her heart race with just a glance? Or that they'd grown and changed since they'd last seen each other?

She decided on an impersonal response. "He made quite an entrance onto the island. He let Santa's sleigh crash into the café."

"So I heard. It's the talk of the town. But that isn't what I was talking about."

"Can I get you some hot coffee?" She knew what her friend meant. "It's really cold out there today. It'll warm you up." Darla grabbed her empty cup from the coffee table and headed for the kitchen.

"Sure. I'll have some."

Darla kept herself busy as she got them coffee. She

noticed the slight tremor in her hands as she reached for the milk. She drew in a deep breath, hoping it would calm her nerves.

When the coffee was ready, she carried both mugs to the couch. She knew she'd procrastinated as long as possible.

After Aster took a drink of the brew, she set her cup aside. "Thanks. That hit the spot." Her perceptive gaze took in Darla's face. "I'm guessing you weren't expecting to see him."

"Not at all. I was chasing after Agnes Dewey because she forgot her purse at the café, and I ran into the street, not thinking about traffic and yet here comes Sam's pickup. It was slick and the truck started sliding. I wasn't sure it was going to stop in time. And then to find that it was Will driving the truck instead of Sam was a shock."

Darla went on to tell her friend about the rest of the evening. "It was a really busy evening."

"Why did you agree to help him fix the sleigh?"

Darla shrugged. She'd asked herself that very question a few times last night. "It seemed like the right thing to do. After all, if I hadn't run out into the street and he hadn't had to slam the brakes, the hitch probably wouldn't have broken, and the sleigh wouldn't have been damaged."

Aster pursed her lips as though giving Darla's answer due consideration. "Even so, why would you agree to work with your ex?"

"Because…" Why had she agreed? It wasn't like the

arrangement was going to be easy for either of them. "It was the right thing to do. But you don't have to worry."

"Oh. Why's that?"

"Because Will is ready to quit the project and we haven't even started." She got to her feet because she just couldn't sit still any longer. She started to tidy up the living room. "It's what he does when things get tough. He quits."

Aster was quiet for a moment. "I take it you think the sleigh can be salvaged?"

"Of course. Sure, it's rusty in places. And it has a big dent that needs punched out. And it definitely needs new cushions and a paint job. But all of that is doable."

"Are you sure?"

Darla stopped from straightening her notebooks and pens on the coffee table. Even her own friend was doubting her judgement. "Of course I'm sure. If I wasn't, do you think I'd have agreed to spend the next two weeks working with Will?"

Aster's brows lifted but she didn't say anything. And Darla didn't have the nerve to ask her what she was thinking because she knew whatever it was, she wasn't going to like it.

"Well, I just stopped over to find out if you were going to join us for some caroling Friday night."

This was news to her. "I vaguely remember them caroling through the town when I was a kid. I remember standing in my grandparents' doorway as they sang 'Joy to the World.'"

"I thought it would be nice to bring back some of the old traditions. So as the town's new events coordinator,

I'm trying to put together groups of people to fill Bluestar with carols on Friday evening. So, what do you say? Will you join us?"

"I don't know." It wasn't the singing that bothered her. She'd been in the church choir growing up—right up until she'd moved away to college in California.

"Please." Aster's eyes begged her. "You have such a beautiful voice. And did I mention that we're having hot cocoa at the mayor's house afterward?"

Darla didn't mention that visiting the mayor's house wasn't a big motivator, seeing as the mayor was her cousin.

But she knew how important the caroling was to her friend, and it was for that reason that she said, "Sure, just let me know where and the time."

Aster told her the details in between sips of coffee. They were all meeting up at city hall at seven o'clock. And from there they'd be assigned streets.

At least this would give her something to do besides sit around and analyze Will's words and intentions. How were they ever supposed to put the past behind them? Was it even possible?

7

12 days until Christmas

The Monday lunch crowd had thinned out.

Darla rushed around The Lighthouse Café's dining room, bussing tables and resetting them so everything was ready for the dinner crowd. She and one other server had managed to stay on top of things. At the height of the tourist season, they could have as many as four servers working at once. But in the colder months, things slowed down considerably. With the snow starting to fly, the locals descended upon the restaurant in greater numbers than during the summer months when the tourists packed the place.

And Pete made sure to feature local favorite recipes. Tonight's special was tavern roast beef. It was a huge draw. Tips definitely would be good that night.

The jingle of the bell over the door alerted Darla to a latecomer for lunch. "Welcome," she said automatically as she raised her gaze and noticed Emma Bell standing there.

Darla smiled at Bluestar's very own Nashville star.

"Hi, stranger. Have a seat anywhere."

"Hi." She returned the smile. "I think I'll have a seat at the counter. I just came in for some hot coffee. Brr... It's cold out there."

"They're calling for more snow this evening."

"I guess we don't have to worry about whether we'll have a white Christmas."

"I think it's a safe bet." Darla finished wiping down the table and made her way to the counter. She placed the dirty dishes in a plastic bin near the kitchen door and moved to grab the coffee pot. "Are you sure I can't talk you into some pie to go with the coffee?"

"As much as I would love some, my waistline won't allow it. I have to fit into my bridesmaid dress next week."

"Not even a cookie? I baked some last night when I couldn't sleep. It's not very big."

Emma's mouth gaped. "Darla, when did you become such a bad influence?"

She took that as a yes for the cookie. Darla reached behind the counter and grabbed a frosted sugar cookie in the shape of a Christmas tree. She placed it on the saucer next to the coffee cup. "Here you go. And I'm not a bad influence... I just like to make people happy."

"Is that how it is?"

Darla smiled and nodded. "How are things with you?"

"I'm living my dream. Not everyone can say that. And when I don't feel like leaving home to go out on the road or I lose track of what city we're in, I remind myself of how lucky I am."

"It must be so exciting to be a famous country singer. I know the entire island was excited when you competed on *Songbird*. Every Wednesday night the town practically shut down between eight and nine. They all called in their votes. Me included."

"And you don't know how much I appreciate it." Emma smiled but it didn't quite reach her eyes. "Thank you."

Darla wondered what was weighing on her friend's mind. She grabbed a cloth and started wiping down the counter, even though she'd just wiped it before Emma had walked in. But to stand there and do nothing just felt awkward.

"It's really great that you were able to arrive early to help with the wedding preparations. Will did the same thing." Why had she gone and mentioned him? Probably because he happened to always be on her mind these days.

Emma's eyes lit up. "And how is that going?"

"What?" She wanted to pretend that she hadn't mentioned Will's name.

"You know what?" Emma smiled again. "How are things with you and Will?"

"Well, that's where it gets interesting."

"Do tell." Her eyes lit up with interest.

Darla told her the story of how they'd almost literally run into each other during the snowy night and the subsequent accident with Santa's sleigh. "It was really quite a night."

"So, that explains the boards over the window."

Emma gestured behind her.

Darla nodded. "They had to special order a big enough piece of glass from the mainland. It should be here in a day or two."

"What I don't understand is, why was Will towing the sleigh across town? And why in the middle of a snow storm?"

Darla glanced around and made sure that the few customers in the café were far enough away not to overhear her. She leaned forward and lowered her voice. "Can you keep a secret?"

Emma crossed her heart with her finger. "I promise. Now dish it up."

"Chief Campbell wants the sleigh restored for the wedding. He wants to whisk your mother away in it after the wedding."

"Aww…" Emma pressed a hand to her chest as her eyes grew misty. "That's so romantic."

"I know. Every time I think romance is dead, someone in Bluestar goes and proves me wrong."

"Don't worry, I won't tell anyone. Have you seen Will since that day?"

This was the part she'd left out. "Well…I was supposed to help him restore the sleigh. But things didn't go well the first day. I think he might have given up on the project."

"Why don't you ask him?"

She shrugged. "I don't think we're in a good enough place to work together."

"You won't know until you give it a genuine effort."

She hated to admit it but Emma was right. So what if things went wrong on Friday. They'd both had the weekend to cool off. It was time to try again.

"I think you're right," Darla said.

Emma smiled. "I have a feeling there's going to be a lot more romance swirling through this town."

"It's not like that."

Emma arched a brow. "Are you sure about that?"

"Positive. Whatever was between us ended a long time ago in San Francisco." Her voice held a note of conviction, but she wasn't quite as convinced as she had been before Will blew back into town. There was unfinished business between them—unanswered questions—but the romance was definitely finished.

"Okay. But maybe give him another chance. You guys were happy once upon a time."

"That was a lifetime ago. A lot has changed since then."

"Has it? Really?" Emma's gaze searched hers. But when Darla silently glanced away, Emma said, "Mom asked me to give you a message. She said we're having a family dinner tomorrow night, and she'd like it if you could be there."

"Me? But I'm not family."

Emma held up her hands innocently. "I'm just the messenger."

And Will would be there. She just couldn't spend more time with him. But how did she turn down Helen, who was nothing but kind to her. She mentally went through her work schedule and realized she had tomorrow evening off. She'd been thinking about stitching the new cushions for the sleigh, if she could find some material.

"Couldn't you make some excuse why I couldn't be there?" she begged her friend.

Emma's eyes gleamed as she smiled. "See, I knew it. You want to avoid Will."

"That..." She was going to deny it but knew she couldn't. "That's true. It's just awkward."

"It'll get better with time." Emma drank the last of her coffee. "But if I tell Mom you aren't coming, she'll track you down herself."

She could imagine Helen doing just that. "Fine. I'll be there."

Emma gave her the details and then headed for the door.

How was it that with every turn she was getting thrown together with Will? She had the feeling the whole island was intent on getting them back together. But it didn't matter how much time they spent together; there was no way to undo the past.

8

Why was he doing this?

Will hammered on the dent with a rubber mallet. He couldn't believe that not only was he refurbishing Santa's sleigh but he was also now doing it alone. He regretted how bad things had gone on Friday with Darla. He'd thought of stopping by the café but he wanted to respect Darla's space.

Even before things had gone wrong on Friday, he'd sensed that Darla would rather do anything than spend time with him. He hadn't come to Bluestar to make her miserable. It was best to leave things the way they were—an uncomfortable silence between them.

But was that what he really wanted? He refused to answer that question. He didn't have the right to want anything more than Darla was willing to offer him. And in this moment, she was freezing him out.

He was lying on the floor beneath the sleigh. He banged on the lower portion of the dent. Nothing happened. He whacked it harder. Some black paint peeled off the side.

"How's it going?"

At the sound of Darla's voice, he jerked upward. His head hit the sleigh. "Ouch!"

The sound of rapid footsteps echoed in the garage. Darla knelt down next to him. "Are you all right?"

He slid out from under the sleigh. As he sat up, he noticed the gleam of worry in her eyes. It warmed a spot in his chest.

"I'm fine." He rubbed the tender spot on his head. "Hard as a rock."

"Are you sure?"

"Positive. What are you doing here?" He stood. "I thought I chased you off for good."

She shook her head. "You aren't that lucky. I said I'd help and I meant it."

He was impressed by her determination. "Well, okay then." He didn't want to rehash Friday's conversation and risk her storming off again. It was best to dive straight into the work. "This is the final dent I need to punch out before I start stripping it down and repainting it. I was thinking a flat black paint, what do you think?"

"Black?"

"Sure. It's already black." He wasn't seeing the problem.

"That's the point. It's black. It needs a change. Something more festive."

"It appears you already have a color in mind."

"I do."

"Are you planning to share?"

"How about white?"

"That's not even a color. It's more like the lack of a color."

"It'll be great. After all, we are getting this ready for a wedding. The body can be all white, and the trim can be gold. And then I can pick out some upholstery material with a holiday vibe."

He sighed. He would have to cancel his paint order at the hardware store. He wondered if it was too late. Even so, he could afford to absorb the cost. But these changes would delay things, as they'd have to reorder the paint. The extra time was something he couldn't afford if they were going to finish in time for the wedding.

He pressed his hands to his waist. "What else do you have on your mind?"

She turned to him with surprise reflected in her eyes. "If this is about the past—"

"Wait. What?" He supposed his question hadn't been exactly clear because there was no way he was digging up their past. It was all best left buried. "No. I meant about the sleigh. What other changes do you have in mind?"

"Oh." Color bloomed in her cheeks.

He'd forgotten how beautiful she was when she blushed. She used to do that when he'd compliment her. It wasn't hard to find ways to praise her, because her beauty started on the inside and worked its way out.

And that was why he'd fallen hard for her in high school. Even though everyone had said they'd been too young to be so serious, they knew one day their lives would merge into one. And so, when Darla said she'd follow him to California, he hadn't seen the problem. He hadn't known his future was going to hit some pretty significant sinkholes.

"Will, did you hear me?" Darla's gaze searched his.

He hadn't heard a word she'd said. He swallowed hard. "Sorry. What did you say?"

"I said I'll help with the scraping and painting."

"Oh. Okay." *Wait*. He was supposed to tell her he was fine working on this on his own. So, why had he agreed to continue to work with her?

She headed to the workbench to retrieve some sandpaper. So much for ending things here. Because if he was to back out, she'd surely know her close proximity still got to him. And he couldn't let her get close to him again. Not after everything.

Maybe he should try again. "I've got this if you have somewhere else to be. I'm sure you would rather spend time with your boyfriend."

"I don't have one." Those words were spoken so softly he almost didn't hear them. "It's not that I haven't dated anyone since we, um, since I returned to the island. I'm just not seeing anyone right now."

There was a flutter in his chest, but he refused to acknowledge it. "I'm not seeing anyone either."

For a bit, a silence fell over them as he finished pounding out the dent while she worked on sanding the rusty runners. Luckily, there wasn't too much rust. And there were no holes. This sleigh had been lovingly cared for over the decades.

Will recalled when he was a little kid watching for the sleigh at the end of the Christmas parade. Santa would throw candy to all of the kids, and Will had always been upfront, trying to catch as many treats as he could fit in his pockets. A smile pulled at his lips as he recalled the past.

"You look happy." Darla's voice drew him back to the present.

"I was thinking about when this sleigh used to be at the end of the Christmas parade. Do you remember that?"

"I do. My grandfather played Santa until he physically couldn't do it any longer."

"Whatever happened to the Christmas parade?"

"I don't really know. But Aster, um, I mean Charlotte. Do you remember my college roommate?"

"I do." Charlotte had always been a good friend to Darla. "But who's Aster?"

"Aster is Charlotte. Her full name is Charlotte Aster. These days she goes by her middle name. It's a long story. Maybe I'll tell you all about it sometime."

"That's got to be confusing for you."

Darla shrugged. "I'm used to it." She stepped back to inspect the progression of her sanding. "Do you think Helen is going to be surprised by the sleigh?"

He nodded. "I think everyone is working really hard to keep it under wraps. I haven't seen my father this excited in a very long time."

"This marriage is going to be a big change for you."

"How so?"

"In the past it was just you and your father for holidays and stuff. Now you're part of a big family."

"It's not like I'm a kid anymore. We won't be living

together."

"Still, when you come back to visit your father, you'll be staying with them and having dinners with your step-siblings. That's got to be an adjustment."

He supposed it would be. He just hadn't let his mind go there. He'd known the Bells all of his life. He was friends with his future step-siblings, so this shouldn't be a hard adjustment. Right?

He shrugged it off. "As long as my father is happy, I'll be fine with it all."

"Even if they sell your family home?"

He hadn't stopped to consider his father selling his childhood home—the place that encompassed so many of his memories of his mother. Within those four walls, he'd learned what true love looked like. Until the end, he'd catch his parents stealing a kiss in the kitchen. Sometimes when he walked in the door, he could still hear the echo of his mother singing a Patsy Cline song.

And when his mother was diagnosed with brain cancer, his father did everything to help his mother. His father had barely slept as he became essentially a single father, sole breadwinner, and caregiver. It was a rough and scary time for all of them.

The thought of someone else living there just didn't sit well with him. But his father hadn't hinted that he would be selling it...so maybe that wouldn't be the case. Still, he'd cross that bridge if they got to it.

"I don't know where they're going to live after the wedding. Dad didn't say anything about it."

"I see. Sorry. I didn't mean to upset you."

"I'm not. I mean it's fine." Though in the back of his mind he was thinking about the possibility of losing the family home, and it didn't sit well with him.

Again, they resumed working in silence. He pounded out the rest of the dent while she sanded the front end. He wondered if the bottom hadn't fallen out of his world way back when if they'd be happily married today. He could see them with two kids and a dog.

But as things stood, that image was an impossibility. So, there was no reason for him to even contemplate it. He was in no position medically to even consider starting anything with Darla.

It was the silence that was letting his thoughts meander to places he shouldn't go. They needed to talk about something that wasn't a trigger to things in the past.

"So, you're still working at The Lighthouse?"

"Yeah. I know my parents are disappointed that I dropped out of college to be a waitress. They don't say anything. But I enjoy seeing and talking with everyone at the café. And the local gossip is fodder for my imagination."

"What does that mean?"

She shook her head. "Nothing."

"Come on, Darla. I know you better than that. What else have you been up to?"

She was quiet for a moment, as though considering her response. "Well, if you must know, I've written a book."

"A book? What kind of book?"

And so, she found herself telling him about the

thriller that she'd completed. "Aster read it. She said I should send it out to a literary agent."

"And did you?"

"No."

"Why not?"

"What if they hate it?"

"But what if they love it?" He was excited for her. Everyone should follow their dreams. "You have to take a chance. Nothing great ever happened without some degree of risk."

She sighed. "It's not like you're taking the risk. I bet you're still working at the same place you were when...well, when I left California."

"And you would be wrong."

She stopped sanding and stood to face him. "Really?"

He nodded. "I thought it was time I went out on my own."

"Wow. That's great. Congrats. Wait. Are congrats in order?"

He smiled and nodded. "The company is new but it's taking off. We're hiring new people all of the time."

"That's amazing." Though she no longer sounded thrilled. She returned to sanding. "I must seem like such a failure to you."

He moved around the sleigh to stand in front of her. "I don't think that at all. I think you know what makes you happy—this island and these people. A lot of people spend their entire lives searching for what makes them happy, but you already know what that is. So, I think you are ahead of most people."

For the first time since he'd arrived in Bluestar, her eyes filled with warmth as she looked at him. "Thank you."

"For what?" He didn't think he'd done anything but point out the obvious.

"Being the Will I remembered. I've missed him—I mean you."

His heart grew two sizes in that moment. She hadn't given him her forgiveness that he greatly longed for but this... It was the next best thing.

He should say something—anything to make this moment less awkward—but his throat was clogged with a rush of emotions. And what did he say to her admission? That he missed her too?

It was true—so very true. He'd regretted breaking off their engagement as soon as he'd done it, but he knew it was best for her. He'd been sick. Very sick. She didn't deserve to be dragged through what he'd endured. He knew what it was to care for and worry over a sick loved one. He'd been that person when his mother had cancer. He didn't want that for Darla.

Her phone went off. "All I Want For Christmas Is You" started to play.

Her face bloomed in all shades of red as she yanked her phone out of her pocket. She silenced the ring. "I need to get this. It's my boss."

Will smiled as he nodded in understanding because he didn't trust his voice.

After the abrupt way he'd ended their engagement—after they'd avoided each other for these past several years—she was still willing to admit that she'd missed him. He blinked repeatedly. Darla was some kind of special.

"I have to go," she said. "Someone called in sick at the café."

He cleared his throat and hoped that when he spoke it wouldn't betray his emotions. "Don't worry. I've got this."

"I'm sorry. I'll be back to work on it tomorrow." And with that she grabbed her stuff and headed out the door.

"Hey," he said. When she paused at the door to glance back at him, he continued. "You should press send on your book. Don't let your dream slip you by."

She nodded and then she was gone.

And then he was left alone with his thoughts. He didn't know if she'd take his advice. For all he knew, she might do the opposite just to spite him. But then again, Darla wasn't a spiteful person. She was sweet, caring, and every positive attribute he could think of. He really hoped her dream would come true.

She couldn't believe what she was about to do.

Hours later Darla hustled home from work. Luckily, there were just light flurries coming down and giving the town a fresh coating. She'd just finished closing up at The Lighthouse but she wasn't tired. In fact, she felt energized. And it was all thanks to Will.

Heat warmed her face when she recalled blurting out that she'd missed him. What had she been thinking to say such a thing? After all, he was her ex. He was the dumper, while she was the dumpee.

She would have to be crazy to let her guard down with him. She still didn't know why he'd suddenly called off their engagement. Back when it'd happened, she'd begged him to tell her. He'd said things weren't going to work out between them. He'd refused to tell her the reason why he'd come to that decision. It was something that had haunted her all of this time. How could you not repeat the same mistakes when you didn't even know what they were?

Maybe that was the reason she'd never dated the same man more than a few times. She always found a reason why they weren't going to work out. These days she was the dumper. Not because she wanted to be but because none of the relationships felt right—felt comfortable. Not like, well, not like the relationship she'd had with Will.

As she admitted that for the first time to herself, she realized how pathetic she sounded. She was longing for a relationship that had blown up in her face and left her all alone with her unfinished wedding plans. With a frustrated sigh, she shoved the thoughts to the back of her mind.

When she reached her apartment, she let herself inside. She took off her boots, coat, and scarf. It felt good to be home.

"Jingle Bell Rock."

Her phone's new holiday ringtone started to play. She couldn't believe she'd had "All I Want For Christmas Is You" playing on her phone with Will

standing there. Her face warmed at the memory.

Darla pressed the phone to her ear. "Hello."

"Hey, what are you up to?" Aster asked.

"I just got home from work. It was a busy night. It felt like everyone was out Christmas shopping."

"So, you didn't spend time with Will this evening?" Aster's voice held a note of disappointment.

Surely her friend wasn't rooting for them to get back together, because that was never ever going to happen. "We saw each other before I got called into work."

"And how was it?"

It was good. It was great. It was almost like old times.

"We were working on the sleigh. I don't know what you want me to say."

Aster sighed. "Nothing. At least you two are able to co-exist."

"It's weird and a bit awkward, but it gets easier the more time we spend together." And then she decided to share a part of their conversation. "He thinks I should submit my book to an agent."

"I told you that all along. So, are you going to take our advice?"

She did have a cover letter and synopsis ready to go. And she'd researched the agents that handled her kind of books. All she had to do would be assemble the email and press send. In the grand scheme of things, it was a small risk. If they hated it, she could just move on. But if she didn't send it, she'd never know.

"Darla, did you hear me?"

"Yes." She started toward her office.

"Yes, as in you heard me? Or yes, as in you're going to submit to an agent?"

"Yes, to both." There was an excited squeal on the other end of the phone, making Darla smile. "And I'm just sitting down at my computer."

"You're really going to do this?"

"I am. I have my list of agents."

"I say submit it to them all at once."

"Really?"

"What have you got to lose?"

According to Will, she had nothing to lose and everything to gain. So, while they continued to talk about Christmas and what festivities they were going to take part in, Darla assembled her cover letter, synopsis, and partial manuscript. One by one she submitted her book.

She had no expectation of hearing back from any of the agents. But secretly there was this little bit of hope that refused to be dimmed. Maybe, just maybe, one of the agents would see promise in her writing.

9

11 days until Christmas

Taco Tuesday with his new extended family.

Will glanced around at the long table at Katrina's Kantina where the Campbells and Bells were seated for dinner. It was definitely going to take him a while to get used to the idea that they were family. He wondered if his soon-to-be step-siblings were having the same problem adjusting.

"You're quiet tonight." Darla's voice drew him from his thoughts.

"Sorry. I'm just getting used to this big family stuff."

"Imagine how I feel about being here and I'm not even family."

She had almost been family—if not for him ruining everything. But what was done was done. He couldn't go back and change things, no matter how much he'd wanted to in those months following Darla's departure from California. Those had been some long, dark times for him.

His father always said what didn't kill you, made you stronger. He didn't feel stronger. He just felt older and maybe, just possibly, a little wiser.

He leaned closer to Darla in order not to be overheard. "You know how Helen is. She likes to include everyone. And you should be here. You're working hard on our special project."

"I plan to work some more on it after dinner."

"Me too."

She smiled at him, and even though darkness had descended over the island, it was like the sun had suddenly reappeared. Her smile filled him with its brightness and warmth. He couldn't believe it, but somehow he'd forgotten how the light would catch in her eyes and make them twinkle. Was it possible she'd gotten even more beautiful with time? Because she was a knockout. And he couldn't believe someone hadn't come along and swept her off her feet.

"Are you sure you wouldn't rather go write some more? I'm anxious to read your book."

She sent him a disbelieving look. "You're just saying that."

"No, I'm not. Honest."

"You'd really read it?"

"If you'd let me."

She paused as though considering his offer. "I took your advice and sent it to some agents last night."

"That's great." He had a really good feeling about this. "Did you tell your family?"

She shook her head. "I don't want to disappoint my parents again if things don't work out."

He was part of the reason she felt that way. Her parents had been excited about their pending nuptials and when it had fallen apart, he heard from his father that her parents hadn't taken it well. It had been a rough time for Darla, and he felt horrible that he'd caused it.

When she should be so excited and sharing her news with her family, she felt she had to keep it to herself. This was all on him.

He reached under the table and took her hand in his. Her skin was soft and smooth just as he remembered. When she glanced at him with widened eyes, he swallowed hard.

"I just wanted to reassure you that good things are about to come your way." Under the table he gave her hand a gentle squeeze and then reluctantly he let her go. "Just keep believing it and don't give up on your dreams."

Her lips parted, as though she were going to say something, but then she pressed them together and instead nodded.

Aster, who was seated next to Darla, asked, "Can you pass the chips and salsa?"

Both he and Darla reached for the basket of chips at the same time. Their hands once more touched. And again, he felt a jolt zing up his arm and settle in his chest. His heart started to beat faster.

He pulled his hand back, allowing her to pick up the basket. He sat there, trying to figure out what he was going to do about his attraction to his ex. Because there was no way he could act on it. He wasn't staying on the island. And he knew she'd never be happy anywhere else.

Then there was the fact that he'd broken off their engagement abruptly. Yeah, that right there was too big of a stumbling block to overcome. Whatever he was feeling was definitely only going one way.

He needed to talk—about something—about anything. It would keep his mind focused on something other than the way Darla made him feel. "Do you remember that little hole-in-the-wall place on Market Street?"

Darla's eyes widened. "I do. They had the best fish tacos. But I have to admit that from the outside I wasn't expecting much."

"But once you stepped through the front door, it was like a world unto its own."

"I know. You would think they'd fix up the exterior."

"But would you have remembered it so vividly if it looked just like every other restaurant on Market Street?"

Darla paused to consider his question. "No. Definitely not. You know, I miss that place. I know that Bluestar has some fantastic restaurants, but I miss those fish tacos. They just did something different with them—something I've never been able to repeat."

"Wait. Did I just hear you say you missed San Francisco?"

She averted her gaze and shrugged. "I guess so." And then she went on to mention some other places she missed, from the theatres to the cable cars. "It seems like forever since I was there."

"I never thought I'd hear you say those words."

Her gaze swung around to meet his. "What's that supposed to mean?"

"It's just that I thought you hated living there."

She shook her head. "I never hated it."

"You never seemed to like it."

She sighed. "I have a confession to make."

He stilled his body, not sure where this conversation was headed. "What's that?"

"It might have been homesickness talking. I couldn't afford to return to visit Bluestar that last year, and I was miserable not being able to see my family."

Why hadn't he thought of that? Maybe because she never said anything to him. Or maybe she had and he'd been so caught up in his own world that he hadn't heard her. He felt awful. If he had known, he'd have done whatever it took to get her home to her family.

"I'm sorry," he said.

Her eyes widened. "For what? It wasn't like you kept me prisoner there."

"No. But I could have helped you get home. I... I didn't know how homesick you were. I should have known—"

"It's not your fault. I should have said something, but I knew you had your hands full with your new job. And I didn't want you to pay for me. I needed to stand on my own."

"Like you're doing now?"

She nodded. "I know being a waitress isn't as fancy as creating apps that change the world or having your own company, but I'm happy."

"I'm glad to hear it. I always wanted you to be happy."

"Even now? After what happened with us?"

"Especially now." With the gates to the past standing wide open, he felt compelled to say something he'd been holding back for much too long. "I'm sorry."

They were just two little words, but they carried so much weight. He felt lighter having spoken them. But would she accept his apology? Had it come too late?

Confusion reflected in her eyes. "We already talked it over. It wasn't your fault that I was homesick."

"No." He shook his head. "I mean I'm sorry about the way things ended with us."

"Oh." Her eyes shuttered, closing him out. She turned her head away as she reached for her margarita and sipped it. "It was a long time ago. I've forgotten all about it."

He knew that wasn't the truth, but he wasn't going to push things. They were slowly finding a way to co-exist, and he couldn't ask for anything more.

"Maybe someday you'll come back to San Francisco." As soon as he'd spoken the words, he realized how it sounded. "You know for a vacation."

She nodded. "Maybe."

He didn't know what to make of what he'd learned this evening. It certainly framed his memories much differently. She hadn't been falling out of love with him—she'd been homesick. If only he'd known…

But if he had known, it still wouldn't have changed things. He still couldn't have been the same man that she'd gotten engaged to. His whole life had changed after a persistent hoarse throat and some other symptoms he'd failed to pick up on.

And all of this hindsight didn't change things. Darla may be friendly with him, but he knew he couldn't let it be more than that. So, he had to be happy that they were on friendly terms again.

10

10 days until Christmas

She loved the holiday.

And even with Will in town, it surprisingly hadn't dimmed her holiday spirit.

Darla finished stitching the cushion on her mother's old sewing machine. Making a new cushion for the sleigh had been a bit more involved than she'd originally imagined because the supplies on the island were limited, and the foam cushion wasn't immediately available in the large size she needed for the sleigh. Luckily, the shop's supplier on the mainland had it in stock, along with some beautiful holiday upholstery decorated with holly berries.

She was stitching the berry-red piping cord to the fabric when her mother walked into Darla's childhood bedroom, which had been converted into her mother's sewing room. "I just found this old photo of your grandfather in the sleigh." Her mother smiled. "He was

so proud of it."

"He made the best Santa. He really had that deep *ho-ho-ho*."

Her mother continued to stare at the photo. "And the belly laugh that made his eyes light up. If I didn't know better, I'd have thought he really was Santa."

"Maybe he was," Darla teased.

Her mother rolled her eyes. "It's a good thing he can't hear you. We'd never hear the end of it."

"Can I see the picture?"

Her mother handed it over. Darla gazed at the image of her grandfather all done up in his custom-sewn Santa suit. Her grandmother had handmade his costumes for him. Yes, he'd had more than one. He'd taken his position as the island's official Santa very seriously. And he looked so happy.

She stared at the sleigh, taking in the original details. She didn't want their makeover to deviate totally from the original look. "Would you mind if I hang onto that photo?"

"Not at all." Her mother nodded at the sewing machine. "How's it going?

"I'll let you be the judge in just a moment." Darla pressed down on the sewing machine foot pedal. She finished stitching the last few inches of stitching. She lifted the presser foot from the material and snipped the threads. Then she turned the material right-side out before holding it out to her mother. "What do you think?"

Her parents ran Spot Clean, the island's only dry

cleaner and alterations shop. Her mother checked the seams. "You did an excellent job."

Darla smiled. "Thank you."

"If you ever want to join me at the shop, you're more than welcome."

"Thanks, Mom. It means a lot, but I think I'll leave the sewing up to you." She thought about telling her mother about the manuscript she'd just submitted to literary agents, but she resisted the urge. The thought of disappointing her parents again would be too much.

"I understand." Her mother sounded a bit disappointed.

Anxious to move on to another subject, she asked, "There's one thing I've always wondered."

"What's that?"

"Why did you put a sewing room in your house?"

Her mother smiled. "You mean why did I transform your room into a sewing room?"

"No. I'm okay with that. It's more like I wonder why you'd want a sewing room at home when it's your day job."

"Ah...I understand." Her mother sat in a cushioned chair by the window. "When you do something you're passionate about, you don't really think of it so much as a job but rather something you enjoy. Isn't that how it is for you at the café?"

Darla shrugged. Though she enjoyed spending time with the people of Bluestar and meeting the tourists, it wasn't something she was passionate about. She wasn't sure she wanted her mother to know that, because then her mother would worry about her happiness.

"I heard you're up for a promotion at the café." Her mother's voice drew her from her thoughts.

"You did?" Then again, why was she surprised? Bluestar's gossip chain was alive and running well.

Her mother smiled. "I'm surprised you didn't mention it."

"I...uh, well, it's not for sure. Pete didn't say if he was going to promote from inside or hire someone new to fill the position."

"Did you let him know you're interested?"

"I mentioned it to him a while back."

"Maybe you should mention it again. Let him know that you're still interested in the position."

It wasn't a bad suggestion. In fact, it was a really good idea. "I'll do that."

"Good." Her mother patted her shoulder. "Your father and I are proud of you. No matter what you do in life. As long as you're happy. That's the important part."

Darla's heart swelled with love. She hoped she'd soon have good news for her parents about her writing, but that was still up in the air.

"How are things going with you and Will?"

It was the question she was asked numerous times a day by her friends. And she was never quite sure how to answer them. What was it they were wanting to hear? That she was miserable being near him? Surprisingly, that wasn't the case. In fact, it was quite the opposite. They were learning to be friends again.

Or was everyone waiting to hear that they were reuniting? Because if that was what everyone was waiting for, they were going to have a very long wait. She didn't want to get back with Will any more than he wanted to get back with her.

There was only one thing she wanted from Will—an explanation. Sure, he'd apologized but it wasn't enough. The generic reason for their breakup just wasn't enough—they'd grown apart and he needed his space. She just didn't buy it. She never had. There had to be more he wasn't telling her.

She could feel her mother's gaze upon her. Darla swallowed hard. "Things are surprisingly going well considering everything. It's not like it used to be. But we're making it work so we can finish the sleigh in time for the wedding." It was time to change the subject. "I still can't believe Helen hasn't caught on to the surprise yet."

"It's so romantic." Her mother exhaled a dreamy sigh.

"What's romantic?" Her father stepped into the room. His cheeks and nose were still red from being out in the nippy weather while clearing the walks.

Her mother turned to him. "How Walter is working to make this wedding so special for Helen."

Her father leaned back against the door jamb. "Mary, is that your way of saying you want me to take you for a sleigh ride?"

"No." Her mother's cheeks pinkened. "I was just thinking how nice it is that no matter how old you get that romance doesn't have to fade away."

Her father's eyebrow arched as he wordlessly approached her mother. And then he swept her mother up in his arms. Her mother gasped. He lifted her off her feet, spun her around, and then dipped her. When she straightened, he kissed her.

"Oh, Ron." Her mother smiled as she pressed a hand to her chest.

He smiled and walked away. From the hallway, Darla heard her father say, "I've still got it."

This was the kind of relationship she wanted. A marriage that lasted decades. A relationship that was open and honest. A union that weathered the storms life threw at you and came out on the other side stronger and maybe each a little wiser. And a husband who loved her and wasn't afraid to show it.

"What are you smiling about?" her mother asked.

She was smiling? She supposed that she was. "Just the way you two still act like teenagers."

"We do not." Her mother smiled. "Your father just gets carried away at times."

"That's because he loves you."

"I suppose that's true. And I love him too."

"You two are lucky you have each other."

The smile slipped from her mother's face. "Don't worry. Someday you'll find the right person. And when you do, he'll break out in dance for no reason at all."

Darla shook her head. "I don't think there's anyone like Dad in my future."

"He doesn't have to be like him. He just has to love you with all of his heart and make you happy."

Suddenly, Will's image came to mind. Once upon a time, she'd thought he was all of those things, but she couldn't have been more wrong. At the first sign of trouble, he'd bailed on her. And she'd never been more miserable in her life.

It had taken months of crying into her pillow at night and pints of Rocky Road ice cream for her to piece her heart back together again. She couldn't go through that again. She wouldn't go through it again. Once was way more than enough.

11

9 days until Christmas

Only a week until the wedding.

And his time with Darla was drawing to a close.

Will sighed as he applied primer to the sleigh. On his first night home, when he'd almost hit Darla and then Santa's sleigh had careened into The Lighthouse Café, he'd thought things couldn't get any worse. He'd been wrong.

Things were getting more complicated by the day. The fact that he and Darla had found a way to be friendly even though the past still stood prominently between them hadn't gone unnoticed by him.

He recalled their conversation at dinner the other night. He had a hard time believing she missed San Francisco. He'd been so certain she'd hated living there. And if his medical circumstances were different, he'd think it was a sign that they should try again.

But that was never going to happen. His cancer diagnosis made it an impossibility. Plus, so much had happened that they could never overcome. And yet he couldn't help thinking about how much he didn't want their time together to end. He wanted to drag out this restoration work for as long as possible, all so he could spend more time with her—so he could bask in the warmth of her smile. Was that selfish of him? Probably. But it didn't make it any less true.

"There you are." His father stepped into the garage.

"I'm just finishing the primer." Will applied the last couple of brush strokes. He set aside the brush and stood, all the while he visually inspected his work, looking for anything he'd missed. "What do you think?"

His father walked around the sleigh. "You've done a great job." And then his father glanced around. "Is Darla still helping you?"

Will nodded. "When she isn't busy working at the café."

"Good." When Will sent him a strange look, his father amended his words. "Have you told her about your remission?"

Will shook his head. "And I'm not going to tell her. Neither are you."

"I don't know why you insist on keeping it a secret. It's nothing to be ashamed of." His father's eyes reflected his concern.

"It's just better this way. We're moving past the breakup. There's no point in dredging it all up now."

"There is if you still care about her. I see the way you look at her—"

"Dad, stop. We're not getting back together." Will rubbed the back of his neck as he took a calming breath. "I just need you to keep what I told you to yourself."

His dad frowned at him. "I won't say anything to her, because it's not my place to, but it doesn't mean I agree with your decision."

"Listen, Dad—"

"Good morning." Darla strolled into the garage. She came to a stop. Her gaze moved between him and his father as they stared at each other. "Did I interrupt anything?"

His father turned to her and smiled. "Not at all. I was just looking over the sleigh, and I have to say that you two have done an excellent job. Thank you so much."

"I haven't done much," Darla said modestly. "All of this"—she gestured to the sleigh—"is Will's hard work."

No way was he taking all of the credit. "That's not true. Darla sanded half of the sleigh."

Color bloomed in her cheeks, but she didn't say anything.

His father nodded. "Well, I just want to say thank you to both of you. And I came out here to remind you that it's time for the final fitting for our suits for the wedding."

"Oh. I totally forgot." Will glanced down at his work clothes with primer splatter on his knees. "I should go change."

"You don't have time," his father said. "We have to get going." And then he turned to Darla. "Could I impose on you once more?"

"Sure. What do you need?"

"Well, Helen had a conflicting appointment and couldn't make it today. She really wanted a woman's opinion about the suits. Could you go with us? I mean, if you have other plans, I totally understand."

"Uh...actually I don't work until this evening." The surprise of the invite was written all over her face. "I don't know how much help I'll be."

"I think it would make Helen feel better to know you supervised."

"Okay, then let's go." Darla sent his father a reassuring smile. "I'm happy to help any way I can."

She walked out the door with his father behind her. Will was left to turn off the lights and bring up the rear. After donning their boots and coats, they set off walking toward Button Up, the island's formal wear one-stop shop.

His father and Darla talked easily. But then again, why shouldn't they? They'd come so close to being family, before it had gone so wrong. Guilt heaped on Will's shoulders. He knew his father had a soft spot for Darla—what wasn't there to love? She was the most amazing woman.

His father said something funny, and she let out a laugh that was gentle and melodic. It was light and lifted his soul so his steps didn't feel so heavy.

It'd be so easy to imagine that the last several years had been nothing more than a horrible nightmare. In this dream, they'd married just like they'd planned. They were a family—a happy family. If only dreams were reality.

♥♥♥

So, this is how things would have worked out if they'd married.

Darla couldn't help but feel she'd been cheated out of something very special. And though she'd been trying to push aside those feelings, it was impossible when she felt herself getting drawn back into Will's life.

How was she supposed to pretend her heart hadn't been shattered—that their dreams hadn't gone up in flames—that their parents hadn't been disappointed? She needed answers—even if she didn't like them. But was Will ready to speak honestly with her?

She wasn't sure, because she hadn't been able to get a good read on him. Sometimes she thought he regretted their breakup, and other times she felt as though he had a wall up between them.

Inside the shop, they were immediately tended to by Tina Dresser, the owner. Their navy-blue suits had just been altered. They were paired with a white dress shirt, blue and white suspenders, and a tie with snowmen printed on it.

The men changed into the new clothes so everything could be checked for the proper fit. Will wasn't smiling but Darla did. She knew how much Will didn't care for dressing up. He used to own only one tie, and it had only been pulled out for weddings or funerals. But she knew he loved his father too much to complain about what he had to wear.

Walter was the first to step back into the showroom, wearing his wedding clothes. He looked quite handsome, but it wasn't the clothes that made him look so good; it was the great big smile on his face. Everyone should be that happy when they were about to get married.

"I can't get this shirt buttoned." Walter yanked at the collar.

"I can help." Darla rushed forward.

She immediately saw the problem—the button was sewn a little too tight. She would mention it to Tina. It took a little effort, but she finally got his collar buttoned. And then she tied his tie for him. The last tie she'd tied had been Will's—it seemed like a lifetime ago.

"There you go." She stepped back and smiled at him. "You look quite handsome. Helen is going to be so happy."

"You think so?" When Darla nodded, he said, "I just want to make it a very special day for her."

Darla's heart swooned. "Trust me, she's going to love the wedding."

Will joined them. She noticed the frown that knit his dark brows together. But when his father turned to him, the frown was wiped away. "Do we need to put on the tie? I mean right now."

She noticed his collar was buttoned. She approached him. "Mind if I check your collar?"

His hand immediately went to his throat, blocking her access. As though he realized his reaction, he lowered his hand to his side. "Why would you do that?"

"Because your father's top button was sewn too tightly and made it hard to button the collar. I just wanted to see if yours needed adjusted too." She reached for the collar.

Will stepped back.

The move surprised her. He wouldn't let her get near him. The other day at the restaurant, he reached out to hold her hand, and yet today he didn't want her checking his collar. What was that about?

It reminded her of what had happened to them in San Francisco. One day they were happy, and the next day he was saying their relationship was over. She didn't like not knowing where they stood from moment to moment.

She glared at him. "I guess you're fine on your own." She turned her attention back to his father, who was adjusting his suspenders. "Can I help you?"

"Aw...thanks. I've got it." He sent her a warm smile, the exact opposite reaction from his son.

Before she could say anything else, Tina entered the room. "And how are things fitting?"

Both men said the suits fit fine. Darla mentioned that the button should be loosened on Walter's shirt. Will was on his own, just the way he seemed to like it.

Darla didn't make eye contact with Will. Maybe his withdrawal was a good thing. It reminded her of exactly why they weren't together. She couldn't trust him not to hurt her again.

"Isn't that right?" Walter glanced over at Will.

Will cleared his throat. "Sorry. Didn't hear you."

"I was just telling Tina that these suits look better than I was imagining."

"Oh. Yeah, they look great."

Darla wondered if Will really meant it or if he was just saying whatever he thought his father wanted to hear. The truth of the matter was that it shouldn't matter to her. She wanted to be anywhere but there.

"It looks like you have everything under control." She spoke directly to Walter.

"Thank you for helping us." He patted her arm. "It means a lot."

"Happy to help but I didn't really do anything."

"You let me know that these clothes will work for the wedding because I don't want anything to spoil that day."

Neither did she. And that meant keeping her distance from Will. "Since I'm no longer needed here, I have an errand to run."

"Oh sure, we understand. Don't we, Will?"

"Um, yeah. And the primer needs time to dry, so nothing more can be done with it today."

Well, okay then. He didn't need to tell her that he didn't want to be around her. The knowledge pierced her scarred heart. She ignored the old but familiar pain.

"You look very handsome." Once again, she focused her attention on Walter. "Helen is a very lucky bride."

"And here I always thought we'd be doing all of this for you and Will." Sadness radiated from the older man's eyes. He blinked and it was gone. "Sorry. I didn't mean to bring that up today."

"It just wasn't meant to be." The words squeezed past the lump in her throat. "I should be going."

And then with her shoulders held in a rigid line and her chin tilted slightly upward, she walked in measured steps to the door. She hoped she'd be able to reach the door before her wall of indifference slipped. She didn't want Will to see the pain he'd caused her. Because in the years they'd been apart, she'd grown stronger. She wouldn't let him destroy the calm, peaceful life she'd created for herself.

♥♥♥

"You are sending her confusing signals."

Will was caught off guard by his father's disapproving tone as they made their way home from Buttoned Up. His father was normally a very laid-back and friendly guy. It took a lot for him to speak his piece.

His father's disapproval was almost palpable. And it added to the guilt weighing on Will's shoulders. "I know."

"Then tell her about your cancer."

Why hadn't he told her he had thyroid cancer? In the beginning it was because he didn't want her to stay with him out of pity, but that didn't explain why he hadn't spoken up since then. "It won't fix things."

"That's where you're wrong. I saw the pained look on Darla's face. She still cares about you—about what happened in the past. This is your chance to put everything right."

He sighed. "And what if I don't want that chance? What if I want everything to remain exactly like it is right now?"

They walked on in silence. The freshly fallen snow cushioned their steps. With the cold day, not many people were out and about. Will would have greatly welcomed a distraction.

He didn't want to upset his father, but there was nothing that could undo the past. There were no words or actions that could undo his prior actions.

"I know you were young when your mother passed, so you wouldn't know that our relationship wasn't always perfect."

Will's chest tightened. If his father was going to reveal some deep dark secret, he didn't want to hear it. "Dad, we don't have to discuss this."

"I think we do. Your mother and I were very different people. We saw life in different ways. You know the saying that opposites attract? Well, that was us. And do you know how we made our marriage work?"

Will shook his head.

"We talked. Even when we didn't want to talk, we talked. When we were upset with each other, we talked. When we totally disagreed, we talked." His father stopped walking and waited until Will faced him. "You stopped talking to Darla."

"I... I didn't want her to stay with me out of sympathy."

"What if she had stayed because she loved you?"

"I didn't want to ruin her life."

"You mean you didn't want her to end up like me?"

Will couldn't say it. He couldn't reveal the way it pained him to see his father go through life alone year after year. He only wanted the very best things for Darla. He didn't want to die and leave her alone.

He'd actually thought after all of the time they'd been apart that she would now have a family of her own. His imagination conjured up an image of Darla with a baby in her arms as she smiled lovingly into her husband's eyes.

Just as quick as that vision came to him, so did the uneasiness in his gut, twisting it up in a knot. He blinked away the thought and instead focused on the here and now.

"My visit to the island isn't about Darla and me. It's about you and Helen. It's supposed to be a happy time. So, can we leave the past where it belongs? In the past?"

His father sighed and the steam of his warm breath escaped. "I'll just say this once and let it go. I think you need to be totally honest with her. It's the only way either of you are going to be able to move forward."

And that was it. That was all his father had to say on the subject. The rest of the walk, his father talked about the wedding and how he'd planned a surprise honeymoon for his bride. They were flying to Europe. Helen had told him that she'd always wanted to see Paris. And so that's where they were going—to get their photo taken in front of the Eiffel Tower.

If Will ever doubted the love between his father and Helen, he certainly didn't anymore. His father was like a young man again, making plans for the future. Will had stopped making plans after he'd ended things with Darla. Sure, he made business plans all of the time—the short-term ones, the twelve-month projections and the five-year plans. But they were all about expanding his business—about making it bigger and better.

But when it came to his personal life, well, he chose not to think about it—think about how empty it had become. Instead, he'd thrown himself into his work—

some might call him a workaholic. To him, it was where he found what happiness there was in life.

He'd heard that after facing your own mortality, you find out really quickly what is most important in life. Some people turned their lives upside down to make it more fulfilling—to appreciate what life had to offer.

He hadn't done that. He hadn't changed his life after making it through all of his treatments. Because he had changed his life at the beginning of his journey. He'd removed the good, the loving, the best part of his life—Darla.

12

8 days until Christmas

Leave it alone.
Don't even go there.

Those were the things Darla had been telling herself ever since Will had backed away from her at Buttoned Up. She hated how things between them would be so good one moment and definitely not so good the next moment. What was he keeping from her?

It had to be something big. She'd never believed his line about how they'd gradually drifted apart. Maybe their communication hadn't been as good as it should have been. But they'd still loved each other.

Things between them had been good until one day they weren't. And before she could figure out why Will had put walls up around himself, sealing her out, he'd ended their engagement.

At first she'd told herself that it was the wedding preparations. She had gone a bit overboard with all of the details. She'd wanted to have just the right venue on Bluestar Island. And she wanted twinkle lights—everywhere. And then there were the favors and the dresses and the list went on and on. It had become too big. By the end, even she wasn't happy. But unlike him, she'd never considered throwing in the towel on their relationship.

As the cold wintery breeze whipped past her, she hunched down in her coat. It was Friday evening, and she was making her way to city hall. Why had she agreed to go Christmas caroling? Oh, yes, it was Aster's idea.

Darla wanted to back out. She was in absolutely no mood to be singing cheerful holiday songs. But Aster was her best friend, and she refused to let her down. Besides it might do her some good to get out and do something to take her mind off of Will.

As she approached city hall, she noticed a crowd congregating near the big Christmas tree. It was all decked out with multi-colored twinkle lights. This particular tree had been decorated every year for her entire life. Traditions ran deep in Bluestar. It was one of the things she loved most about the town. It was reliable and consistent. Not much changed in Bluestar.

She searched through the sea of faces until she spotted Aster, the mastermind behind bringing caroling back to the town. And by the large turnout, it appeared Aster's idea was well received. Darla smiled. Her grumpiness washed away. Maybe this wasn't such a bad idea after all.

She moved toward Aster, who had a clipboard in her hands. "How's it going?"

Aster beamed. "Great. The caroling had a bigger response than I was expecting. I'm just putting everyone in groups."

"Where do you want me?"

"Would you mind being in my group? I thought it'd be fun if we could do this together."

"Does that mean Sam backed out?"

Aster nodded. "He had to fix something on the goat pen. He felt really bad about missing it, and he almost came with me until I assured him you would be here."

"Let me guess. Dash is up to his old tricks again."

Aster nodded again. "He certainly keeps life interesting."

"Well, don't worry. I'll be happy to sing off-key with you."

"Hey…"

Darla sent her friend a playful smile. "Okay, I'll sing off-key, and you will sing perfectly."

"Not nearly as good as my future sister-in-law."

"I bet you could give Emma a run for her money."

Aster rolled her eyes. "Keep on dreaming."

Darla's gaze moved through the crowd. "Speaking of which, where is Emma?"

"She's over with her family." Aster pointed toward the bottom of the steps to city hall.

"And where are we to go?"

"Well, that's the thing—Helen insisted we be a part of her group."

Somehow during this holiday season, she kept getting drawn into Helen's world, which was also Will's world. She was hoping to put some distance between them. It just wasn't right that two exes were constantly thrown together.

"Aster, I don't think—"

"Aster!" Someone called out. "Can you help Birdie and Betty figure out what group they're in?"

"Sorry." Aster looked apologetic. "I'll just be a minute. I'll meet you by the steps."

As people moved to their designated group, Darla hesitated. What were the chances that Will would participate in caroling? Not very good. He'd always claimed he couldn't sing.

And then Helen spotted her and waved her over. Darla hesitated. Still, she didn't want to do anything to upset the woman who had been nothing but kind and friendly to her. So, Darla plastered a smile on her face and moved toward the Bells.

"I'm so glad you could make it," Helen said. "I know with the holidays that you're working a lot of hours at the café."

She was hoping those many hours would translate into a promotion. And then her thoughts strayed to the manuscript she sent out to the agents. She hadn't heard anything back from the agents. She was hoping to hear something before Christmas

"I requested the evening off. I didn't want to miss this." Her gaze moved through the crowd. When she found Will wasn't among the familiar faces, she breathed easier. "This is going to be a lot of fun."

"I'm so glad Aster is planning all of these events. We haven't been caroling in ages. And afterward, we're having hot cocoa and Christmas cookies at my house. I hope you'll come."

Darla had originally planned to go back to her place and write, but she supposed it could wait for a bit longer. "Thank you. That sounds really nice."

"Ladies and gentlemen." Aster stood at the top of the steps in front of city hall. "Thank you so much for joining us this evening. Do each of you have a song booklet?" She held up the printed book. "If not see me right after I finish here."

"Am I too late?"

The familiar voice came from behind her. Darla didn't want to turn around. She didn't want to acknowledge Will's presence. But as he moved in beside her, Will's presence was impossible to ignore.

"I thought you didn't sing," she said.

"I don't but I can lip sync with the best of them." He winked at her.

"Really?"

"Shh…" Darla gestured toward Aster, who was still giving out instructions.

And so, Will stood silently while Aster completed her little speech. Darla couldn't believe Will had showed up this evening. This was so unlike the Will she used to know. She wondered what else had changed about him. Not that she was going to ask. She didn't want to know.

When Aster joined them, they set off to their designated street. On the way Will said, "I don't have a song book?"

Aster looked flustered. "I ran out of them. I'm sorry. I don't even have one for myself. I know, you can share with Darla."

Darla turned her head and shot her friend a dirty look. Why was everyone trying to push them together? First, it was Helen. Then it was Will's father. And now it was her best friend.

The last thing Darla wanted was to get closer to Will. Because every time she was near him, her heart started to beat faster—just like it was doing now.

She handed Will the booklet. "Here. You can have it. I know all of the songs by heart."

"Are you sure? I don't feel right taking your booklet."

"I'm positive."

The group stopped in front of the first house. As the group started singing, Emma went to the front door and knocked. A minute later the door opened, and an older couple appeared in the doorway. Their faces lit up with joy. And that was what Darla focused on—not the fact that she wanted to get as far from Will as she could get before other people got the wrong idea about them spending time together.

As they walked, Darla slowly made her way to the other side of the group. She could feel Will giving her strange looks, but she ignored him. They might be working on the sleigh together, but that didn't mean they had to spend all of their time together.

And so, they made their way up Surfside Drive and back down the other side. By the time they'd finished, Darla was feeling a bit hoarse. The hot cocoa would feel good against her scratchy throat, but she decided to quietly slip away and head home.

When the group turned left toward Helen's house, Darla went in the opposite direction. She glanced back to find Aster hadn't noticed her disappearance, as she was deep in conversation with Emma. She was probably inviting the island's biggest star back for another performance. Aster always had one event or another on her mind. And come the beginning of the year, she'd be the town's full-time events coordinator.

Darla's steps were quick. She turned a corner. Her escape was successful. She slowed down and sighed. She could go home, put on her pajamas, and curl up on the couch with her laptop.

"Darla, slow up!"

Her body stiffened at the sound of Will's voice. The last time she'd seen him, he was talking to his father. Why would he follow her?

She kept moving, pretending she hadn't heard him. Maybe he'd give up and turn back. Could she be that lucky?

He wasn't walking away.

Will had felt terrible ever since he'd pulled away from Darla at Buttoned Up. It was just a protective instinct. If she had unbuttoned his shirt collar, she would have seen his surgical scar.

She'd caught him off guard, and he hadn't handled it well. And since then, Darla had been more distant than ever. He didn't know if he could fix things, but he wanted to try—he needed to try.

Because he'd just gotten Darla back as a friend, and he wasn't ready to lose that connection yet. He'd forgotten how much fun they could have together—well, when Darla wasn't walking away from him.

He didn't know what he could say to fix things. He knew the truth about his illness might score him some sympathy, but that wasn't what he wanted. In fact, it was the last thing he wanted.

"Darla, slow up." When she didn't acknowledge him, he picked up his pace. "I know you can hear me."

Her shoulders slumped ever so slightly, and her pace slowed. She didn't turn around, but she made it easier for him to catch up with her.

"You seemed surprised to see me at the caroling," he said, trying to chip through the ice between them.

"I know that singing isn't your thing."

"So, Aster didn't say anything about me attending."

Darla's head turned to him. "She knew you were going to be there?"

Maybe he shouldn't have said anything, but it was too late now. "I didn't know it would upset you. In fact, I didn't know we were going to be in the same group."

"I can't believe everyone is trying to get us back together."

"Maybe not everyone. I didn't notice Pete say a word about seeing us together."

"That's because unless it's café business or something to do with his family, he's oblivious to everything else."

It wasn't much but at least he had her speaking to him. "I just want you to know that I didn't put any of them up to it."

"I know."

"How do you know?"

"Because you were the one that ended things in San Francisco, so why would you have people try to set us up?"

"Maybe I came to my senses and realized I'd let the best woman in the world go." What had he gone and said that for? It was the truth, but he'd never intended to say it out loud.

When she glanced at him, she arched a brow. "Nice try but I know the truth."

"The truth?" His pulse quickened as his mind started to race. "How do you know?"

"I figured it out. You don't think I'm that stupid, do you?"

He resisted the urge to press a hand to his neck just to make sure that his scar was still covered. He swallowed hard. "I…I don't know what to say."

"There's nothing to say. I know you met someone else and dumped me." Her voice was icy cold, making the below-freezing breeze rushing past them seem rather balmy.

"Darla, what are you talking about?" Because he had no idea where she'd gotten such a ridiculous idea.

She came to a stop outside of her apartment building. Beneath the street lamp, she turned to him. "Will, it's okay. Time has passed. I'm not going to freak out if you tell me the truth."

"What truth?" There was no way he could let her go on living with this fallacy in her mind. "Darla, I swear to you that there was never anyone else."

Her gaze searched his. "You're serious?"

"Very. I never ever thought of cheating on you. No one can compare to you."

A series of emotions flickered in her eyes as she digested that information. He didn't know where it would leave them, but he hoped it would make her feel better.

"Thank you for clarifying that. It…it means a lot."

He nodded in understanding. "I'm sorry people keep pushing us together. I swear I had nothing to do with it. But I would understand if you wanted to stop working on the sleigh." As soon as he said the words, he knew it wasn't what he wanted. The more time he spent with Darla—the more he wanted to be with her.

Darla hesitated. The look in her eyes said she was torn about what to do. "We started the sleigh together. I'd like to finish it together, if it's okay with you."

For the first time that evening, he smiled—a genuine smile. "I'd like that."

She returned his smile. "Good. I'll see you tomorrow morning."

"Sounds good." They firmed up their plans and then he said, "Well, I'll see you in the morning."

"Good night." She turned and headed toward the building.

He waited until she stepped inside before he turned and left. He never thought the evening would end the way it did.

How did Darla get the idea that he'd cheated on her? He felt awful that all of this time she'd been thinking he would hurt her like that. He knew after getting the cancer diagnosis that he'd become increasingly withdrawn.

And maybe he'd picked the wrong way to handle things, but he hadn't wanted Darla to stay with him out of sympathy. When she'd agreed to marry him, he'd been healthy with a future of possibilities. But that diagnosis had changed everything for him, and in the beginning, he didn't know how things were going to turn out. And the last thing he wanted was to tie Darla down to a sick man—it wouldn't have been fair to her.

But he had no idea that she thought he was cheating on her. He could honestly say he'd never been tempted by anyone else. Darla was everything he'd ever wanted in a life partner. She was sweet, thoughtful, and had a heart as big as the world.

13

7 days until Christmas

It was the best time of the year.

Saturday morning, Darla found herself smiling more than normal. She was so happy to learn that Will hadn't cheated on her or traded her in for a new model. But it had caught her so off guard that she'd been stunned. And then she'd been relieved to the point that her brain had stuttered.

Because if her mind had been cooperating, she might have asked him why he ended things so abruptly. Could it really have been that he'd felt they'd drifted too far apart? There had been a lot going on at the time. There had been his new job, her college classes, and the wedding plans. There had been very little time for them to be together, but she'd never fallen out of love with him—not at all.

She lifted her head and glanced over to where Will was applying gold paint to the trim. They'd searched the internet until they'd found stencils to use to decorate the sleigh. Neither of them were that artistic, and they'd

decided stencils would provide the help they'd need.

"How's it going?" he asked.

She glanced down and realized she had to move faster if they were going to finish the detail work today. "I still have a ways to go. How about you?"

He leaned back and surveyed his work. "I'd say I'm a little more than halfway done. I can help you when I finish."

"That's okay. I'll get it done."

"How about I get us some coffee."

She smiled. "I like the way you think."

"I'll be right back." He set aside his paint and went inside the house.

While he was gone, she set to work painting as fast as she dared. She didn't want to go too fast and mess up the sleigh. They'd worked too hard to get this far. And Will was going to coat the entire sleigh with a clear coat that would help protect it from the elements.

She couldn't wait to see her parents' expressions when they saw the finished sleigh. And then there was the bride—Helen was going to be so surprised. The groom had even lined up two horses from a local farm to pull the sleigh. A dreamy sigh escaped her lips.

"Everything okay?" Will's voice drew her from her thoughts.

"Yes." Usually, she'd stop there but now that they'd found a new comfortable relationship, she decided to share her thoughts with him. "I was just thinking about how romantic the wedding is going to be. Helen is so lucky. Walter loves her so much."

Will nodded. "My dad is crazy about her. I haven't seen him this happy since, well, since my mother was alive."

Darla finished painting a swirl, then she straightened. When she turned to Will, he held a cup of steaming coffee out to her. "Thank you."

He looked at her as though he wanted to say something but he wasn't sure if he should.

"Go ahead." She wanted to know what was on his mind.

"What?"

"You want to ask me something, so go ahead. I think we've reached a place where we can talk openly."

He cleared his throat. "I, well, I was wondering, do you ever feel like you missed out by not finishing your degree?"

She hadn't been expecting that question. "I don't know." She hadn't given it a lot of thought since she started on her writing venture. "But I never like to leave things unfinished."

"So, if you got the chance, you'd finish it?"

"I suppose so. Why?"

He shrugged. "I just feel bad that I caused you to drop out."

Oh. That was it. "I could have stayed and finished. It wasn't you that drove me away from San Francisco."

His eyes widened. "It wasn't?"

She shook her head. "I was really homesick for the island. I missed my parents. I missed the café. I mean, I like San Francisco but it just isn't the same as Bluestar."

"So, you'd never move back there?"

"It's not in my immediate plans, but I wouldn't say never. I'd just make sure I could come back to the island on a regular basis. Why? Do you think I should go back to school?"

He shrugged. "That's totally up to you. I think you should do what makes you happy."

"Do you know what would make me happy?"

"No. What?"

"Us finishing this sleigh."

He smiled. "I think that's doable."

Her heart fluttered in her chest. She chose to ignore the sensation. After all, this wasn't the beginning of anything between them. In fact, soon it would be the end. Because once the wedding and Christmas were over, he'd be jetting back to the other side of the country.

She grabbed her paint brush to get back to work. It was best to keep things as they were and not even think of how nice it'd be for him to hold her in his arms again. It'd been so long since she'd pressed her cheek to his strong chest and heard the *thump-thump* of his heart. The paint brush slipped from her grasp.

She jerked her meandering thoughts up short as she rushed to clean up her mess. She had to stay focused. Nothing good would come of thinking about what would never be.

14

5 days until Christmas

He was shoe shopping.

Monday afternoon, Will felt a frown pull at the corner of his lips. He was not a shopper. The things he needed, he ordered online. It saved him the time and effort of having to track down something that not only came in his size but had the style and color he liked.

But his father had declared that morning that he didn't have a decent pair of shoes to get married in. When Will had mentioned that the place they were renting their suits would have shoes, his father told him he wasn't getting married wearing someone else's shoe. Will had considered asking him why it was okay to wear someone else's suit but not someone else's shoes. However, Will decided to refrain.

"We need to talk." His father made his way along the recently swept sidewalk.

"Okay." Will had absolutely no idea what his father

was talking about, but he remembered as a kid when his father used those words, it was never followed by anything good.

His father approached the men's store and pulled the door open. Wordlessly, he stepped inside. Will followed him. His father headed toward the shoes in the back.

Will tried to imagine what his father wanted to talk about, but he had no idea. Was it something about the wedding? Was his father considering calling it off?

"What do you think of this one." His father held up a dress shoe with ties.

"It's fine. But maybe you should pick out a few pairs to try on and see which one is the most comfortable."

"Good idea."

Will flagged down a sales associate, and his father pointed to four different shoes. He wanted black in a size eleven.

When the associate moved to the back room, Will asked, "What did you want to discuss?"

His father sat down in one of the two chairs. "I want to know why you don't like Helen."

"What?"

"I don't know if I can get married if I know that it makes you unhappy."

"I like Helen. A lot. And I'm really happy for the both of you."

His father stared into his eyes. Worry lines etched his face, making it look so much older than he was. "If you're so happy for us, then why do you look so miserable?"

"I do?" That was news to him. He never imagined what he was feeling about his own life had translated to his face. He felt really bad about it. When his father nodded, Will said, "It has nothing to do with you and Helen. I swear."

"Then what is it?"

Just then the sales associate returned with three boxes of shoes. The one pair they didn't have in his father's size. It was the pair with the ties that his father had picked out first. But his father didn't seem concerned about the shoes. Once the associate moved on to another customer, his father turned to him.

"I don't know," Will said but it was a cop-out. He knew what was bothering him. He was uncomfortable with putting it into words, but he had to try and put his father's mind at ease. "I just feel like I'm missing something in life." He sighed and slouched back. "I'm even considering selling the business."

"Why would you do such a thing? That business is everything you ever dreamed of. Is it that you're homesick?"

Will shook his head. "Don't get me wrong, I love the island, but my life is in San Francisco."

"I understand. Everyone has to find their place in life. I miss you, but I want you to be happy. But selling the business—I just don't think that's the right move."

"Back before I had the business, I thought it would make me happy. Now I find that I was happiest before the business was a reality. Maybe it was the challenge of building something unique—something that was all my own. And with the business completely operational, it just isn't the same. Whatever it is, somewhere along the way, I lost what drove me—what made me happy."

His father arched a brow. "Have you ever really thought about what truly made you happy?"

"I don't know. I guess it was the challenge of creating a new business from the ground up—pushing myself to create something no one else had ever done."

"Or it's the fact that you had someone in your life to share the journey." His father lowered his voice. "Have you told her about your remission yet?"

Will shook his head. "It wouldn't be fair to tell her now."

His father leaned back in his chair. "You know when your mother was sick, there was no one else I'd have wanted to care for her. It was an honor that she trusted me and leaned on me."

"But I saw how it drained you. By the time we lost Mom, I was afraid we were going to lose you too."

His father reached out and gripped his forearm. "I'm sorry you had to go through all of that, especially at such a young age."

"I… I just didn't want to put you or Darla through the worry."

"I understand. You were watching out for us. But I think you lost something very special when you ended things with Darla."

Could his father be right? Was the fact that Darla wasn't in his life anymore the reason his life had lost its luster? Was it because she wasn't there to share the details of his accomplishments or setbacks?

Will sighed. "It's impossible to get back what we once had."

"Nothing is impossible. You just have to want it bad enough."

Did he want Darla back? Before he could contemplate the answer to that question, he shoved the thought aside. All of that was in the past. Even if he did want Darla back, she had moved on with her life. There was no way she'd want him back. And he couldn't blame her.

♥♥♥

Christmas was almost here.

And the sleigh was almost fully restored.

Darla told herself she should be excited. But she'd somehow lost her holiday spirit. It had suddenly dissipated. And for the life of her, she couldn't figure out why. Her tree was trimmed. The presents were bought. And as of last night, they were all wrapped. So, it wasn't any of that.

Everything was on track. By the end of the week, it would all be over. Will would be jetting off to the West Coast. The thought brought a pang to her chest. Was that it? Was she bummed because soon Will would be gone?

"Darla, can we talk?" Pete stood in the doorway that led to the kitchen. His facial expression was nondescript.

She shoved aside her thoughts of Will. She had more immediate problems. Pete didn't call meetings unless it was important. This couldn't possibly be good. Not a chance.

She swallowed hard. "Uh. Sure. Just let me get some coffee for table four, and I'll be right with you."

"I'll be in my office."

She nodded in understanding.

But she didn't understand. Not really. Did it have something to do with the sleigh breaking the window? If so, why did he wait so long to say anything?

Her gaze moved toward the new picture window. Ethan had replaced it. And he had done a wonderful job. You couldn't even tell that anything had happened. But the truth was that everyone on Bluestar Island knew Santa's sleigh had crashed into The Lighthouse Café. She supposed she had been kidding herself to think there wouldn't be any fallout.

She made sure all three occupied tables were taken care of and then not having a legitimate reason to delay this any longer, she made her way back to Pete's office. It was just off the kitchen. The door stood ajar.

She knocked on the door jamb. "You wanted to see me."

"Yes. Come on in and have a seat."

Her stomach shivered with nerves. Had someone made a complaint? She studied her boss's face as he reviewed a supply receipt. He looked so serious, not like the smiling, easy-going Pete she'd come to know through the years.

She didn't want to lose her job. She liked it there. She loved being a daily part of the community. She knew what was going on—who got engaged—who was fighting—who was moving in and who was moving out. The job was so much more than serving food. It was congratulating accomplishments, sympathizing the rough times, and just being there.

"Pete, I know that accident with Santa's sleigh was partially my fault, and I just want to say again how sorry I am. It won't happen again—"

"Whoa. Slow down." He lifted his reading glasses to rest them on the top of his head. "You aren't in trouble."

"I'm not?"

"No."

She blew out the pent-up breath she'd been holding. "Then why did you call me back here?"

"To tell you that I am promoting you to assistant manager." He smiled at her.

"You are?" *Really?* She'd thought for sure that after the accident, she'd lost this opportunity.

Pete stood and walked around his desk. He held his hand out to her. "Congratulations."

She placed her hand in his. He gave it a firm shake before releasing it. A smile pulled at her lips. "Thank you so much."

"It's I who should thank you. You are reliable and go above and beyond. We'll go over the details of the position after the holidays."

After she thanked him again, she returned to the front of the café. She couldn't stop smiling. She couldn't wait to tell Will.

She halted the thought as soon as it came to her. Why in the world would she want to tell him? It wasn't like they were a couple or anything. Not even close. But if the subject were to come up, it wasn't like she wouldn't share the news with him.

The café phone rang. She grabbed it. "The

Lighthouse Café. How may I help you?"

"Darla, is that you?" the male voice asked.

"Yes." She wasn't quite sure who it was but the voice was familiar.

"This is Walter Campbell."

"Oh, hi. What do you need? Is it something to do with the wedding?"

"In a way. Helen and I were hoping to spend tomorrow together—away from all of the wedding preparations. But I already promised Will that I'd go with him to get a Christmas tree. I will understand if you're busy, but I was wondering if you had some time, if you'd be willing to go with him to the tree farm."

She knew the wedding plans had taken over their lives. The thought of them taking the day away from Bluestar was romantic. And she was more than willing to help—even if it meant spending more time with Will.

"Tomorrow, I finish working after the lunch crowd. Would that work?"

"Yes, that would be perfect. Thank you, Darla. I really appreciate this."

"No problem. I'm happy to do it. Just go and enjoy yourselves."

When they disconnected the call, she wondered if she'd made a mistake by agreeing to spend more time with Will. Perhaps she should find someone else to go with him. But she knew that most of her friends would still be working.

But how bad could it be? After all, she loved getting a Christmas tree and decorating. It would be fine. She would just ignore the shiver of excitement she felt when she was around Will. Because absolutely nothing was going to happen between them.

15

4 days until Christmas

'T was the time to decorate.

They'd been so busy getting ready for the wedding that they'd barely done any decorating for Christmas—including buying a Christmas tree. Will didn't mind so much, but his father said it just wouldn't be Christmas without a tree in the house.

And with the sleigh almost completed, there was no reason they couldn't go get a tree this morning. But his father was nowhere to be found. Will could only guess his father was spending time with his bride-to-be.

Will smiled as he pressed *send* on yet another business email. This wedding was really going to happen. Life was about to permanently change...for the better. Christmases would no longer just be him and his father. There would be the Bells and Darla. Wait. Not Darla. Why would he include her? They were not and would not be back together.

Still, if he accompanied his father to get a Christmas tree, it'd keep him from dwelling on his prior conversation with Darla. If he stayed busy, he wouldn't be tempted to go to her. Because what would that accomplish?

Sure, she'd looked at him differently after she realized he hadn't betrayed her. He couldn't deny the warmth in her eyes had lifted some of the weight from his shoulders. But not all of it was gone. There was still a lot he was holding back.

Through the years he'd told himself that he'd been protecting Darla from the pain and worry of going through the cancer treatments. It wasn't until this point that he realized he'd really been protecting himself.

He hadn't wanted Darla to look at him with pity like he was less of a man. That would kill him on the inside. She wouldn't have meant to hurt him, quite the opposite. Yet little by little, everything would have changed between them.

What would he accomplish by telling her all of this now? It was best just to keep things casual and return to California as soon as Christmas was over. She'd go on with her life, and he'd go on with his—just like they'd been doing.

He checked the time. It was ten minutes till one. His father had left early that morning, and Will had no idea where he'd gone. But his father wasn't one to miss an appointment or meeting, especially seeing as though he was the one who had set up the plans to have lunch and head out to the tree farm at one.

While his father was gone, Will had applied the clear

coat to the sleigh. While it dried, he decided to get some work done. He'd been working each evening, but with all of the interruptions, he hadn't gotten enough done. Being the CEO of his own tech company meant the bulk of his time was spent responding to emails and reviewing reports. He didn't get to write code anymore—there was never time. And besides he'd hired some young fresh-out-of-college employees to do that work for him.

His assistant was at the office, making sure to keep him up-to-date on everything that happened around the office—office being a loose term. His leased space had pool tables, foosball, and pinball machines because he worked with creative people. And he was one of them.

He knew their jobs weren't robotic. At times when they hit a snag, they had to be able to walk away from the problem in order to let their subconscious come up with a possible solution. He'd done it a lot when he'd developed the WC Book Journey app. His favorite go-to choice had been a handful of classic pinball machines he'd picked up along the way. By giving his mind a break from the problem, he was able to unravel the situation and develop an alternative solution.

He'd adopted his experiences into his new company. He'd made common areas with couches and snack foods. It was like one big hangout area with conference rooms discreetly tucked in the corners and cubicles on a different floor for those times when you didn't want distractions. It was everything he'd wished he'd had when he'd graduated college and started his first job.

Will opened the next email in his long list. He wasn't

happy that it was a Human Resources issue. He hated those the most out of all of his duties. Because the HR issues that reached his desk were always the difficult ones—the ones that fell somewhere in a gray area.

He read the email once and then twice.

Buzz. Buzz.

He glanced at his phone, which was sitting next to his laptop. Will had commandeered the dining room table for a temporary desk. Caller ID let him know his father was on the line.

"Dad, where are you? I thought we were going to cut down a Christmas tree."

"Well, see, there's a problem with that. I'm on the mainland."

"Mainland? What are you doing there?"

"I needed some time alone with Helen. Nothing serious. It's just that we've both gotten so caught up in all of the wedding preparations that we haven't had any time alone together. We had to unplug and step back for a bit."

Will could understand that. He couldn't remember the last time he'd seen his father so excited about anything quite like he was about this wedding. And it was true that he hadn't seen his father and Helen just hanging out like they used to do. When Will used to come home for a visit, he'd find them cooking together in the kitchen or sitting on the couch streaming a new show on television.

"You do what you need to do," Will said.

"Thanks. But we still have the problem about the Christmas tree. We're running out of time. Would you mind going to get one without me?"

"Me? I don't know anything about picking out a tree."

"Don't worry. I figured you wouldn't want to go alone, so I asked someone to go with you."

Immediately he was suspicious. "Who?"

"They should be there shortly. I'll see you tonight."

And with that his father disconnected the call.

Surely, his father wouldn't have sent Darla. Will rushed to the front window and stared out at the white golf cart, but its winter covering was fogged up, and he couldn't see its occupant.

Will stuffed his feet into his boots and slipped on his winter coat. He wondered if he should grab a saw. To save time, he dashed into the garage and grabbed one that was hanging on the pegboard above his father's workbench.

Seconds later he was out the door and headed toward the awaiting cart. A light snow put a coat on the sidewalk. He unzipped the door opening and a bunch of warm air rushed out past him. Inside he found Darla sitting behind the steering wheel. He hesitated.

This isn't a good idea. Not a good idea at all.

"Don't just stand there letting out the warm air. Hurry and get in."

He climbed inside and zipped up the door. "I just want to say that I didn't know anything about this."

"It's okay. I spoke to your father." She pressed on the accelerator, and off they went toward the north end of the island where Bluestar's only Christmas tree farm existed. They delivered some trees to town but a lot of the locals, including his father, liked to go pick out their own tree and cut it down.

"You don't have to do this," Will said.

"When your father asked, I said I would."

"You don't have to go with me. I can do this on my own."

She let off the accelerator. The cart began to slow. "Yes, I do. I told your father I would help out. I won't go back on my word to him."

"Are you sure?"

"Yes, I am."

"Okay then."

Inside the golf cart, Darla had a propane heater situated in a cup holder. For such a little heater, it certainly put out a lot of heat. However, it wasn't enough to thaw out the frosty atmosphere.

He didn't know what to say to Darla, so he said nothing at all. He stared straight ahead at the roadway that at one point had been plowed before fresh snow drifted over it in places. It was beautiful, like a Christmas card, but not nearly as beautiful as the woman sitting next to him.

He chanced a glance at her. She could still take his breath away. But it wasn't just the pink in her cheeks, her full red lips, or her green eyes; it was something much deeper. It was the way she made time for the people around her. It was the way she kept her word—even if she had other things to do. It was the way she listened to people with genuine interest that made them feel special.

Even though he'd started his own company and was a big name in his sector of the world, he wasn't worthy of Darla. That thought sat heavy on his mind for the remainder of the quiet ride. When they reached the Christmas tree farm, they found there were quite a few other residents there.

"Seems my father isn't the last person to put up his Christmas tree." When Darla didn't say anything, he asked, "When did you put up your tree?"

"On Black Friday, just as soon as I took down my Thanksgiving decorations."

He smiled. "I see some things don't change."

She smiled back. "No, they don't."

Darla had decorated for Christmas on Black Friday for as long as he'd known her. She used to say that the shopping could wait, but the decorations couldn't. She would decorate her entire apartment, and then she'd visit his place and help decorate it, although not to the extent she decorated her own. The memory kept the smile on his face.

Their boots crunched over the snow as they made their way to the hillside with trees from the petite to the towering. Signs gave the general direction to the trees by their height. His father didn't usually do extremes, so a six-foot tree would do. And trees of that size were midway up the hill.

"This is nice," she said.

He glanced over at her and found her smiling at him. His heart picked up its pace. He couldn't resist returning the gesture. "Yes, it is."

"So how big of a tree were you thinking?"

"About six feet or so."

"So, a small tree."

He sent her a playful frown. "That's not small. Small is the little artificial tree I put on the table in my apartment."

Her brows rose. "That is small. But at least you have a tree. I can remember when I had to drag you out to buy an artificial Christmas tree. What happened to it?"

He shrugged as he glanced away. "It seemed too big for just one person."

"You could have shared it with someone."

Christmas had always been something he'd done with her. He'd never wanted to share the holiday with anyone else. But he didn't want to admit it to her. He didn't want her to think he'd pined away for her all of this time, because that wasn't true. He'd dated other people—it just so happened that none of them could compare to her.

"It just never worked out." Desperately wanting to change the subject, he said, "Look over there." He pointed to the left. "I think those trees are the right size."

And so, they trudged through the snow to the designated trees. They split up as they searched for just the right tree for his father. Will studied the shape of a tree first. If it looked well-shaped, then he checked to see if it had a straight trunk.

After looking at a dozen trees, he found a potential candidate. He knelt down on one knee to check the base of the trunk. And then he felt something hit him in the back. Icy cold snow splatted the back of his head and fell

into the collar of his jacket.

He jumped to his feet and spun around. Another snowball hit him in the chest.

His gaze landed on Darla as she laughed. Merriment twinkled in her eyes. She reached for more snow.

"You wouldn't." He glanced around to see if anyone was close to them. They were alone. In that short amount of time, he was pelted with another snowball. "This is war."

"Bring it on." She ran behind a pine tree.

He gathered snow and pressed it into a firm ball. When he glanced up, he didn't see Darla, but he knew she wasn't far away. He made another snowball. Armed and ready for action, he went in search of her.

Finding her a couple of rows over, he snuck up on her. She was making a stash of snowballs. He nailed her shoulder. She spun around and launched one at him. He jerked out of the way and it flew by him.

Laughter and smiles abounded as the snowballs flew through the air. They'd been nothing more than kids the last time he'd had this much fun. He never thought he'd get to share this sort of moment with Darla ever again.

But he reminded himself to keep things casual. Darla deserved someone better than him—someone who wasn't broken—someone who would be happy to live their life there in Bluestar—someone who wasn't him.

16

It was an amazing day.

Darla couldn't remember the last time she'd smiled so much or been so cold. More than one of those snowballs had crumbled on impact, sending icy cold snow down her back. With the tree chosen, cut, and strapped to the top of her golf cart, they were headed home.

In fact, they'd just pulled up in front of Will's childhood home. And Darla didn't want this moment to end. She was reminded of how much she missed times like this—missed the fun she'd had with Will.

"We better get the tree inside," she said. "We're only half done."

"Half?" He sent her a puzzled look.

"Yeah, you know, the tree has to be decorated."

"But you don't have to do that."

She smiled at him. "I don't mind. In fact, I'm looking forward to it."

She'd have Christmas decorations up year-round, except that would take the specialness away from them.

And so, each year just after the New Year, with much reluctance, she packed up all of her decorations.

The chance to decorate another tree and check out all of the ornaments from Will's childhood excited her. And secretly she enjoyed the fact that they would spend more time together. Not that she was expecting anything to come of it. How could it? He lived in California, while she lived there on the island?

But still, now that they'd talked—now that she knew he hadn't cheated on her—that perhaps it was her fault they'd drifted apart by her not talking to him about her homesickness, well, it changed things. She'd been holding in a lot more anger toward Will than she'd been willing to admit to herself. With the anger and pain gone, she felt as though her feet were floating above the ground.

Together, they untied the tree from the roof of her golf cart and carried it into the house. Will immediately built a fire in the fireplace, and Darla moved to the kitchen, surprising herself by remembering her way around it. She made them hot chocolate with some mini-marshmallows that Will found in the back of a cabinet.

For a bit they sat by the fire with a blanket draped over her shoulders while they sipped their cocoa. Neither spoke as they took in the moment. It was quiet and comforting. It felt...well, it felt normal—as though they'd done this many times before—because they had.

She chanced a glance at Will as he read some emails on his phone. The firelight played across his handsome face, from his warm brown eyes down his straight nose to his temptingly kissable lips.

He turned his head to her.

She jerked her gaze away as heat warmed her face. "Um, we should get started with the tree. Do you know where the decorations are?"

"In the attic."

And so, they retrieved the boxes. Once they located the tree stand, Darla held the tree trunk straight while Will laid on the floor and tightened the screws to hold it in place. When she released the tree, she moved off to the side to inspect their work. Not too bad.

She reached in her back pocket and retrieved her phone. She selected some Christmas songs and then turned up the volume. "That's better."

He got to his feet and shook his head.

"You surely aren't going to complain about holiday songs when we're about to trim the tree, are you?"

He hesitated as he stared deeply into her eyes. Her heart *thump-thumped* rapidly. She felt as though she were being drawn into his gaze. She could feel reality slipping away. In that moment, it would be so easy to forget the past—forget the way he'd broken her heart.

He glanced away, breaking the moment. And Darla was left wondering what had just happened. She'd told herself she was over Will—she'd finally gotten him out of her system. Or had she?

"I would never deny you listening to Christmas music. I know how much you love it."

She smiled. "You could sing along too."

He shook his head. "I don't think so."

"You used to sing. Why are you now lip syncing?"

"It was a lifetime ago when I sang." His voice was deep, full of some emotion that she couldn't quite identify. "Since then I've realized that I can't carry a tune."

"Oh, come on. I know you have a great voice."

He shook his head. "It's not going to happen."

"But please. I'll put on your favorite Christmas song."

His brows rose. "I have a favorite?"

She nodded. "You do."

"How come I don't know this?"

"Maybe you have selective memory."

"I think I have a great memory. So, if I have a favorite song, what is it?"

"The Mr. Grinch song."

He opened his mouth as though to argue the point but then silently pressed his lips together. He shrugged. "What can I say? It makes me laugh. But I'm not singing it."

She clasped her hands together and pleaded with her eyes. "Pretty please."

He gave a firm shake of his head. "No."

"Why not?"

"Darla, drop it." His firm tone brooked no argument. He turned his back to her. He gathered their empty mugs and took them to the kitchen.

Darla stared in the direction he'd gone. What had happened? She'd thought they'd been having fun and then suddenly Will was upset with her. Maybe she had taken her teasing a little far. She shrugged. He'd get over it—whatever it was.

Not wanting to ruin this moment, she let the subject drop. He might not be willing to sing but that didn't mean she couldn't sing. And so, she sang along as she opened one cardboard box after the next, taking inventory of Christmas decorations. And then she figured out a plan for decorating the tree.

As time passed and Will was still avoiding her, she realized she should apologize. Yes, that definitely sounded like a good idea because trimming the tree alone was no fun at all.

Darla moved to the kitchen doorway. His back was to her as he stood in front of the coffeemaker. "Hey." She paused, hoping he would turn to her, but when he didn't, she said, "I'm sorry. You don't have to sing."

He was silent.

"Will you come back and trim the tree with me?"

"Uh, yeah. I'm just getting us some coffee."

"Okay. I'll start putting on the lights."

And so, she pulled out the strands of lights. She plugged each string into the outlet to make sure they worked before she strung it on the tree. She'd learned the hard way to check the lights before stringing them on the tree. Because once the lights are on the tree and the ornaments are neatly hung, it's a lot harder to find a burnt-out bulb.

"How's it going?" Will asked.

"The good news is that all of the lights work. The bad news is we bought a really fat tree, and I'm having a hard time stringing the lights by myself." That was a bit of a stretch because she could have done the lights by herself, but she didn't want to. "Would you mind giving me a hand?"

"I think I can manage that so long as you take this." He held out the mug of coffee to her.

Was this some sort of peace offering? If so, she happily accepted it. "Thank you."

Time passed quickly as they decorated the tree. They laughed. They talked. They reminisced. And Darla found herself smiling until her cheeks hurt. Oh, how she'd missed these times with Will. If only it could last forever…

17

He didn't want this moment to end.

Not ever.

Will basked in the warm glow of Darla's brilliant smile. He'd forgotten just how good it felt to spend time with her. Even before they'd broken up, they'd lost this fun and easy connection. Had that loss of easiness in their relationship played into his decision to end their engagement? Because as much as he wanted to blame it all on his illness, he knew there had been more. He'd just never analyzed it before. He just knew it was the right thing to do in the moment. Perhaps. It had been more like a tsunami of emotions and bad luck.

But he didn't want to think of any of that now. He just wanted to do or say anything that would keep Darla smiling.

It was dinner time by the time they hung the last ornament. They both stepped back from the tree and stared at their accomplishment. He had to admit that Darla created the prettiest Christmas trees without them being over the top.

"It's perfect," he said with sincerity.
"We need to do one more thing."
"What's that?"
"We need to draw the curtains."

His eyes widened as he realized what she was up to. "Good idea."

Together they drew all of the curtains, darkening the room. The tree, lit up in a multitude of festive colors, sent a soft glow over the room. Every lightbulb was lit. A glance at Darla let him know she was pleased with their efforts.

"What do you think?" she asked.

"I think you should be a professional decorator. It looks fabulous. And so does the rest of the room." He turned around, letting his gaze slowly take in the entire room. He paused when he got to the mantle. It was there that something caught his attention. He stepped forward and picked up a holiday decoration. "I remember this."

"You do?"

"Of course. You gave it to me for Christmas when we were in eleventh grade." He stared at the ceramic snowman with the plastic black top hat glued to his head and a knitted red scarf around his neck.

She stepped closer to him to stare at the knickknack. "The hat doesn't exactly fit him, but a snowman has to have a top hat."

"I know." He smiled as he recalled Darla's explanation. "It's where he gets his magic."

She smiled brightly. "Exactly. So, you were listening to me."

"Of course I was. It wasn't every day the most beautiful girl in school made me a Christmas present."

Color flooded her cheeks. "I didn't exactly make it. I painted the figurine."

"And then you took the time to find him a top hat and a scarf."

"The scarf I made."

He tilted the figurine and glanced at the bottom, where Darla had put her name and the year. This was when he first realized just how special Darla was to him. She had been his best friend, and when he'd imagined his future, he saw her in it. So how had he lost track of all of that?

He turned to her. "This is when I knew I was in love with you."

"You did?"

He nodded. "I didn't know where life would lead me, but I knew I wanted you to be a part of that future."

He stared deep into her green eyes. His heart pounded. It was as though the years of separation had never happened. It was as though they had gone back in time.

His gaze dipped to her lips. They were pink and glossy. Her mouth was so tempting. What would she do if he were to kiss her?

He lowered his head. It had been so long—too long. And though he had lied to himself all of this time, he could no longer deny that he missed her. In truth, he'd missed her as soon as she'd walked out of his San Francisco apartment. Getting through the cancer treatment without her had been the toughest time in his life.

But to be there with her, it was like a dream—a dream come true. If he touched her, would she disappear? As though in response to his thoughts, his arm rose. His fingers tingled with the need to feel the softness of her cheek—to make sure this was real.

His hand rose until it was mere inches from her face. Would it be possible to erase the past several years? Would Darla want to start over?

She stared into his eyes, but he was unable to read her thoughts. As his hand reached out to her, she didn't back away. She didn't move at all. And then the back of his fingers grazed her cheek. The breath hitched in his throat.

He leaned toward her as though drawn to her by a magnetic force. His heart beat so hard he could no longer hear his own thoughts.

"I've missed you." Darla's voice wavered with emotion.

He was suddenly jerked back to reality. He stepped back. What had he been thinking? He blinked a couple of times just to make sure he hadn't dreamed all of this, but she was still there, staring at him with a confused look on her face. He drew in a deep breath and blew it out. He really messed up this time.

The sound of her voice—or was it her words—whatever it was, had snapped him out of the spellbinding trance. What was he doing? There was no way they could go back and recreate what they'd once shared. They weren't the same people. They'd both grown and changed during their years apart.

"Will?" Darla stepped closer.

He took two steps back. "This"—he gestured between them—"it can't happen."

He saw the light in her eyes go out. For a moment, she didn't say anything. "Will, what's going on? Why do you run hot and cold?"

He raked his fingers through his hair. He turned away from her, unable to stand the pain written all over her face. "It's just talking about the past. It's brought up a lot of old feelings."

"Look at me."

He didn't want to face her again. He didn't want to see how he was about to hurt her for a second time. He didn't deserve her—not at all.

"I can't... We can't do this. It'll never work." He turned to walk away.

"That's it?" Surprise rang out in her voice. "That's all you're going to say?"

He paused. The weight of her words was heavy on his shoulders. He turned back to her. "I'm sorry."

"Not sorry enough or you wouldn't be repeating the past."

"What's that?" Not that he wanted to know—but rather he felt as though she wanted him to ask.

"Walk away without an explanation." Pain threaded through her voice.

"I already told you, this isn't going to work."

"That's not an explanation. I want to know why it won't work? I deserve to know."

"You know why this"—he gestured to the two of

them—"won't work."

"No, I don't."

Why was she pushing this? Did she want things to work out this time? If she only knew the truth—if she knew about his cancer diagnosis—she would change her mind. Wait. That was it.

He had to tell her about his cancer. If she knew, she'd understand that he wasn't the same man she'd once loved. He had changed in so many ways.

With it being December, darkness came calling early. Only the lights on the Christmas tree illuminated the room. Will took comfort in the shadows.

He sank down on the sofa and slouched back. Where did he even begin? "Things weren't right between us before we broke up."

"You mean before you ended things."

"Yes, before I ended things. You were caught up in the wedding plans, but they didn't seem to make you happy. And when I suggested we have a smaller wedding, you didn't like that idea either."

"I never thought I'd have to plan our wedding alone. My mother was on the other side of the country, and you were constantly working."

"I didn't mean to leave you alone, but it was a new job. I wanted to prove to myself that I had what it took to make it in business."

Darla sat down next to him, leaving a respectable distance. "I didn't realize how much pressure you were under."

"And I didn't realize how homesick you were. But

that isn't the whole reason I ended things. Remember when my voice was hoarse, and we thought maybe it was a cold that was lingering?" When she nodded, he said, "Well, I noticed a small lump in my neck. I went to the doctor and was diagnosed with thyroid cancer."

"What?" Her eyes widened as she gaped at him. He could see in her eyes a million emotions filtering through them.

"It's why I pulled away from you at Buttoned Up." When confusion reflected in her eyes, he knew what he needed to do. He pulled down the collar of his white high-collar knit sweater, revealing the horizontal scar on the front of his neck.

Darla gasped. It took her a moment to gather her composure. "Oh, Will, I'm so sorry. I had no idea."

He adjusted his sweater. "Not many people know. It's the way I wanted it."

"But you're all right now?"

"Yes. I have to go back for regular checkups."

"And this is why you ended our engagement?"

He nodded and remained quiet for a moment. He understood some of what she was feeling because he'd been in shock after the diagnosis. "It was right after I learned about the cancer that I knew I couldn't marry you. You didn't sign on to be with a sick person. You had your whole life ahead of you and I...well, I didn't know what, if any, future I had."

Tears welled up in her eyes. "Why would you think that? I loved you. I would have been there for you."

He shook his head. "It was something I had to do on my own. I watched my father care for my mother when she was dying. It was so hard on him. I... I loved you too much to put you through the pain and hardship of being my caregiver."

She paused as though digesting the gravity of his words. "That's why we shouldn't have gotten married. Because you weren't willing to trust me—to believe that I loved you enough to be there for you through the good and the bad—not because you had cancer." She stood. "You had no right to predict my level of love for you. And it was wrong of you to decide what's best for me." She shook her head in frustration. "I'm beginning to wonder if I ever knew you at all." She grabbed her things and strode out the door.

"You know me better than anyone," he said to the closing door.

He should have gone after her. He should have told her how sorry he was and how much he regretted his decision. But he couldn't undo the past. And she was so hurt that he was certain she wouldn't hear a word he said.

This time when she'd walked out the door, he had a feeling it was forever. The easiness that they'd found with each other this holiday season had ended with the thud of the door closing. And he had never felt more alone in his life. Because it wasn't until Darla was gone that he acknowledged one simple truth—he still loved her.

18

2 days until Christmas

He'd had cancer.

That startling thought circled round and round in Darla's mind all night. How had she missed Will being so sick? How could he have not told her?

Feeling as though the walls were closing in on her, Darla strolled through Bluestar with no particular destination in mind. She just couldn't sit still. She was filled with anger at Will for keeping all of this from her—from stealing away her choice of whether it was too much for her. She was hurt that he hadn't trusted her to handle this. And she was sad to know the man she'd loved had gone through something so scary without her.

And then her boss called. She was late for work. She was never late for work. Honestly, she hadn't thought of anything but finally knowing the truth of why Will had ended things.

She rushed to the café. She apologized profusely. But the night hadn't gotten any better. She mixed up orders, spilled the coffee, and basically had her worst night ever. She was so grateful when it was time to go home.

She lay on the couch that night, staring at the Christmas tree lights. But she didn't really see the lights. Her mind had gone back in time to San Francisco as she searched her memories for all of the clues she'd missed. At some point during the long night, she'd dozed off.

Buzz. Buzz.

The morning sunlight streamed in through the window, momentarily blinding her. Darla reached for her phone that had fallen on the floor. She squinted to see the caller ID through her sleep-hazed eyes. It was her mother.

She pressed the phone to her ear. "Hey, Mom."

"Happy Christmas Eve." Her mother's voice was joyous, the exact opposite of how Darla felt at the moment. "Are you going to be here soon? I was hoping we could get the Christmas pies baked early since we have the wedding later today."

She had forgotten all about the Christmas pies. It was the last thing she wanted to do today, which was saying a lot because she was always the first to jump at a holiday activity. But she couldn't let her mother do all of the baking on her own.

"I'll be over as soon as I grab a shower." Darla yawned and stretched.

"Sounds like you had a late night. Is everything all right?"

"I'll be fine as soon as I get some coffee in me."

"Are you sure you want to help? I can manage on my

own."

"Of course, I want to bake." She sat upright. "I'm just on my way to the shower. See you soon."

"Okay. Love you."

"Love you too."

Darla disconnected the phone and grabbed a cup of coffee, which she carried to the shower with her. She had to pull herself out of this slump because she refused to ruin her mother's holiday. Even if this Christmas felt more miserable than the one after their breakup.

They were over. Again.

At least that's the way it felt to him.

Will slouched down in his winter coat, trying to avoid as much of the icy sea breeze as possible. He let out a yawn. Hopefully, the cold air would help wake him up. He'd had a restless night filled with nightmares of Darla breaking up with him and marrying someone else.

When he'd woken, his immediate instinct was to call her. He'd gotten as far as grabbing his phone and pulling up her number before he realized he didn't know what to say. *I'm sorry* didn't seem like enough.

"Hey, bro."

The familiar voice came from right behind him. There weren't many people out and about on that crisp morning. Was it possible they were speaking to him? Will glanced over his shoulder to find Emma approaching him.

"What? Is it too soon for the bro part?" Her gaze searched his.

He shook his head. "Not at all. I'm proud to be your

brother."

"You don't look too happy about it." She arched a brow. "What's going on?"

He shrugged. He'd been holding it all in for so long it would feel good to talk to someone. But he wasn't sure Emma was the right person to talk to about his problems.

"Will, you know you can talk to me. We didn't get a chance to talk last night at the rehearsal dinner, but I noticed Darla's absence. What's going on?"

"Do you mind if we walk and talk?"

"Not at all. It's too cold to stand still."

"I was headed to Main Street to pick up some new socks for my father. He decided none of his socks were good enough to get married in."

Emma smiled. "So, he's got wedding jitters too?"

He nodded. "How's your mother?"

"The same. She just sent Hannah and Aster to the florist for some more flowers. She decided we didn't have enough for the reception."

"But she still wants to get married, right?" The breath caught in his lungs as he waited for the answer.

"Definitely. She loves your father a lot."

"He feels the same way for her."

"So then why do you look so unhappy?"

He thought he'd hid his misery over what had happened with Darla. "Why does everyone keep saying that to me?"

"Maybe because there's something weighing on you. I'm a good listener, if you want to talk. If not, I'll just be your quiet companion."

He shouldn't talk about it. He should just let the scene with Darla go. It wasn't like talking about it was going to change anything. But he knew he wouldn't be able to let it go any time soon. And he didn't want it to ruin this big day for his father. Maybe he should vent a little.

When he opened his mouth, it all came spilling out. He didn't want to leave Bluestar with things so messed up between him and Darla. He wanted to go back to that easiness they'd worked so hard to find.

"Did you ever think that you want more than friendship?" Emma asked.

He shrugged. "Even if I did, I messed that up years ago. And now, well, now I'm not the same person. It just wouldn't work. I have to focus on my business. It makes me happy."

"Be careful about investing all of your happiness into your career. It doesn't provide an interesting conversation over dinner. And it's not there on those long lonely evenings to watch a movie and share a pint of ice cream with. Not that I would know much about any of that."

"Sounds like you know a lot about it. Aren't you happy in Nashville?"

She shrugged. "It has it's really good moments, and then there are the other times."

"Does this mean you'll be moving back to Bluestar?"

She immediately shook her head. "My future isn't on the island. Doesn't mean I won't make a point of visiting more often, but Nashville is now home to me. Maybe it's just all of the touring I've been doing lately that's getting to me. But we were talking about what's bothering you. Are you sure you don't want to smooth things out with Darla?"

He rubbed the back of his neck. "Even if I did, it could never happen. Not now. Not after everything."

"How do you know unless you talk to her—I mean really talk to her. Tell her you still care for her."

He shook his head. "It wouldn't be fair. I'm not the same person."

"And neither is she. You've both grown and changed. Give her the chance to make her own decision instead of you trying to make all of the decisions for her. What do you have to lose?"

Emma was right. Things were so bad between them that if he didn't try to fix things, he didn't think Darla would ever speak to him again. And that thought didn't sit well with him. Not at all.

He wanted to go to her, but he couldn't. His father needed him. But after the wedding, he would speak to Darla. He would lay it all on the line, including the part where he still loved her.

Two mugs of coffee later...

Darla made her way through the lightly falling snow to her parents' house. As she came up the walk, she noticed the Christmas lights already lit; after all, it was Christmas Eve. The roof was trimmed in twinkle lights. The porch was decorated with snowmen. And in the big picture window in the front of the house was the Christmas tree all lit up. Darla had no doubt where she'd gotten her enthusiasm for Christmas.

When she stepped in the front door, she could already smell something all buttery with a hint of cinnamon baking. She shrugged off her coat and placed her boots off to the side. Then she followed her nose to the kitchen.

"And what do I smell?"

"Oh, just some nut horns. You know how your father loves them for the holidays."

"I thought he liked nut rolls."

"He does. He likes anything with nuts in it."

Darla nodded. Will was the same way. As soon as the thought came to her, she pushed it aside. She was not going to think about him today.

"Did you get the sleigh finished?" Her mother started to roll out a pie crust.

Darla began putting together the ingredients for a pumpkin pie. The last thing she wanted to do was talk about anything that had to do with Will. "Yes, it's all done."

"That's wonderful. I know Walter must be excited. Just wait until Helen sees what he has planned." Her mother turned the dough. "With them off on their honeymoon, Will will be alone, or are you spending Christmas with him?"

"No." The answer came out faster than she'd intended.

"Really? But I thought you two were getting along so well."

"Not anymore. In fact, we're not really speaking at the moment."

"Oh." Concern reflected in her mother's eyes. "What happened?"

"I finally learned why he called off our engagement. All of this time, I thought there was another woman. I couldn't have been more wrong if I had tried."

"That's good, right? I never imagined Will would cheat on you. He was always crazy about you."

And then a thought came to her. If Will had told his father about the cancer, how many other people knew? "Did you know he had cancer?"

"What?" Her mother's eyes widened in surprise. "Are you sure?"

"I'm certain. He told me himself. So, you didn't know?"

"Of course not. I would have told you if I had known. But why didn't he tell you back then?"

"That's what I wanted to know. When I asked, he said he didn't think I could handle the news. He didn't want me to be stuck with a sick husband." Her voice faltered. The thought of Will dealing with it all alone tore at her heart. "He'd rather go through it alone than to lean on me and trust that I'd be there."

"Oh, Darla, I'm so sorry."

"Me too." She stirred the pumpkin puree a little too fast and some spilled over the side.

They worked quietly for a bit. When they placed two pumpkin pies in the oven, her mother said, "Back when your father and I were dating, he suddenly broke up with me."

"He did?" She'd never heard that before.

"Your father had signed up for the Army."

"I knew he was in the Army, but I didn't know you two broke up over it."

Her mother nodded. "I don't like to talk about it, but maybe it's time you heard this story. Before your father left for bootcamp, I confronted him. I was so angry with him. I didn't understand why he'd done this because I still loved him."

"What did he say?"

"That he would be gone for a long time, and he didn't want to put me through a long-distance relationship. This only made me angrier. I told him that was a decision I should make. He seemed surprised that I would want to wait around for him. Granted, I wasn't happy he was going to be gone for so long, but I already knew he was the only guy for me. So, if I had to wait for him, I would do it."

"I had no idea that any of that had happened."

"We don't dwell on it, because it was a difficult time for both of us. But in the end, we stayed together and got married as soon as his time was up."

Darla knew her mother was trying to encourage her not to give up on Will, but it was too late for that. "I'm glad it worked out for you and Dad, but it's not the same for Will and me. He wasn't away in the military. He was right here in the States. He could have picked up the phone or visited me any time he wanted, but he didn't."

"And yet I think you still love him. I don't think you ever stopped."

Darla couldn't deny her mother's words, so all she could do was shrug.

"I think you need to talk to him again. Lay it all out there. Was there a reason he didn't feel he couldn't turn to you? Was everything as good between the two of you when he ended things as you want to remember?"

She tried to remember the days leading up to their breakup. They'd had words, not exactly a fight, but they'd snipped at each other. She'd been feeling the stress of the wedding and though Aster had been there, she'd been busy with her own life. And somehow the wedding plans had morphed into something much bigger and more expensive than either of them had planned.

Her parents had needed to replace machinery at the dry cleaners, and the finances had been tight. Darla wasn't about to ask them for the money to fly home, and everything she'd earned at her part-time job had gone toward the wedding.

She hadn't wanted to burden Will since he was working so hard at his new job, and so she'd become more withdrawn. That was when the trouble had begun. She hadn't trusted that he could handle her homesickness, and if she told him she thought the big wedding was a mistake, she'd worried he would think she didn't want to marry him.

Maybe Will wasn't the only one guilty of not being honest and upfront. Without communication, they didn't have much of a relationship. And he was right for calling off the wedding.

But were things different now that they were older and perhaps a bit wiser? She'd like to think so. She wouldn't know until she spoke to Will.

And then an idea came to her. "Mom, do you know if any stores are open today?"

"I think some of them are open until noon. Why?"

"I just realized I have a Christmas present to buy."

Her mother smiled. "Then you better get going."

"But there's more baking to do."

"Don't worry. I've got this. You go do your shopping and when you get back, there will still be plenty to do. Now get going."

"If you insist—"

"I do." Her mother smiled brightly. "I have a feeling this is going to be a very special Christmas."

Darla didn't argue with her. She hoped her mother was right.

19

The day was a blur of activity.

Will had never seen his father so excited and so scatter-brained. He wondered if that was the way he would have been if he and Darla had gotten married. It was amazing to witness that kind of love. It was like his father was twenty years younger.

And as much as Will longed to speak to Darla—to straighten things out, he just couldn't abandon his father—not now—not right before his wedding. But he would speak to Darla today—as soon as he could sneak away.

"I can't find my tie." His father came rushing into the living room in his suit. "I've been looking for it everywhere. And it's time to go to the church. We can't be late. Helen would never forgive me."

Will smiled at his father. "Relax. Everything is going to work out."

"That's easy for you to say. You have your tie." He gestured to Will, who was all dressed and ready to head to the church.

"And you have yours too." Will pointed to the tie that was folded and tucked into his jacket pocket.

"Oh. Yes. Right." His father reached for the tie. He lifted his shirt collar, but his trembling hands made tying it difficult.

"Stop. I'll do it." Will stepped up to his father and took over.

"You know Darla will be at the wedding."

"I know."

"I have no idea what happened between you two, but everyone in town is abuzz with suspicions." His father's voice filled with concern.

"I'm not surprised."

"She left here yesterday in quite a huff."

"Dad, now isn't the time for this talk. It's your big day."

"But I'm worried about you. You keep pushing away your happiness."

"I am happy." Maybe his life wasn't what he imagined it would be, but it could definitely be worse.

"You'd be happier if you'd let down your guard with Darla and let her back in your life."

"She doesn't need me messing things up for her. She just got a promotion at the café. And she has some other things in the works."

"That's all good, but it won't take the place of love." He sighed. "You need to understand that even though your mother is gone and I'm getting remarried that your mother gave me a gift by sharing her life with me. Not just the good parts but the bad ones too. She made me a better person. She showed me that I'm stronger than I thought. You stole that chance from Darla."

He knew his father meant to help, but it was just making Will feel worse. "Dad, I wanted to protect her because I loved her."

"Just promise me you'll talk to her before you leave the island."

He knew his father wasn't going to let this go. And Will refused to be responsible for ruining his father's wedding. He expelled a resigned sigh. "If I promise to speak to her, will you stop worrying about me and focus on your big day?"

His father smiled. "Yes. And there's one more thing."

"What's that?"

"Helen and I have done a lot of talking. After the wedding, we've decided to live in her house, as it is bigger, and as she put it, it has more room for the future grandbabies to come visit." His father gave him a pointed stare. "So, I wanted to know if you'd be interested in buying this house?"

"Yes." The answer came with absolutely no hesitation. This house was a piece of his past and present. And now he had a feeling it would play an important part of his future.

"Are you sure? I don't want you to feel obligated."

"No. I mean I don't feel obligated. And yes, I want it." He couldn't wait to tell Darla. There were so many things he needed to say to her. "Now let's get you to the church on time."

As they put on their coats, his father said, "Someday, I hope I'm doing this for you."

"Let's not jump ahead."

"A father is allowed to dream."

Will shook his head. Who would have guessed that his father was a romantic at heart? Ready to change the subject, Will said, "Just so you know, I've made arrangements to have the horses and sleigh waiting for you two outside the church. It will deliver you to the reception at the community center."

"Perfect." His father's eyes shimmered with unshed tears. "I just want you to know how much I love you. And I'm so happy to be able to share this day with you."

"I love you too, Dad."

And then they were off to the church. Being that there was snow on the ground, they opted to take his father's cart. All the while, Will thought over what his father had said. Should he really take a chance with Darla? What if his cancer came back?

Maybe he should do as Emma had suggested and let Darla answer those questions for herself instead of him trying to answer them for her. His gut shivered with nerves. Yes, that sounded like a good suggestion. But what would she say?

♥♥♥

Her gaze darted around the church.

Will was nowhere to be seen.

Darla clutched her beaded purse. She knew her chances of catching him before the ceremony would be slim to none. But all of this waiting was getting to her. She wanted to tell him how she felt before she lost her nerve.

As such, she took a seat midway back, and Aster soon joined her.

"This is so exciting," Aster said. "This is my first Christmas Eve wedding. And I really like it."

"It is gorgeous." There were candles at the end of each pew with holly berries and ribbons. "How is Sam doing with all of this change?"

"He's really happy for his mother. I think it took each of the siblings a bit to come to terms with their mother moving on, but they all like Walter so that really helps."

Darla nodded. "The bride and groom seem so happy. I wonder if I'll ever be that happy."

Aster leaned closer. "You would be that happy if you and Will would give in to your feelings for each other."

"Shh..." Darla glanced around, making sure they weren't overheard.

"What? Everyone in town knows something is going on with you two."

"Did you say anything to anyone?"

Aster shook her head. "You know me better than that. But you were spotted walking in the snow yesterday, and then there was your disastrous shift at the café. The whole town is abuzz. They can't decide if you two are fighting or if you're getting back together. I have to admit that I'm wondering too."

Darla inwardly groaned. "Don't they have anything more important to talk about?"

"You know Bluestar. They love a good romance?"

"But it's not a romance. At least not yet."

Aster gasped. "Not yet? As in you want to get back together?"

"Shh... I haven't talked to Will yet. But my mother helped me realize that our breakup wasn't all one-sided. It took two to let things fall apart."

Aster's lips formed an O. "Hopefully, it'll take two to put it back together again."

That was what Darla was hoping too. But she had absolutely no idea what Will was thinking and that worried her.

She squeezed her purse with a very special Christmas present inside. Her shopping trip had taken longer than she'd anticipated because she had no idea what to get Will. She'd started at the men's shop, but a shirt or sweater just didn't seem quite right. She needed something more personal. And then she'd visited the card store because they always had cute small gifts. But again, she couldn't find just the right item. However, when she'd stopped by the Lily Pad craft shop, they had the perfect gift.

Just as the piano started to play, someone sat on the other side of Darla. She turned her head to find Agnes Dewey, all dressed in black. Her gray hair was pulled back in a bun, while her pale face was devoid of makeup. Instead of a smile, she wore a frown. Didn't the woman know this was a wedding not a funeral?

"I can't believe they're really going through with it," Agnes said.

"Why wouldn't they?" Darla said in defense of the happy couple. "They deserve all of the happiness they

can find."

"You, of all people, should know that love doesn't last."

Darla knew the woman was referring to her and Will, but what Agnes didn't know was that her love for Will had lasted. She'd just been in denial all of this time. "It will last."

She wasn't so sure if she meant it about the bride and groom or about her and Will. Would it be so bad if it were meant for both?

Walter, Will, and Sam stepped to the front of the church. A hush came over the crowded church. Darla's heart swooned at the sight of Will all dressed up. His hair looked to be freshly trimmed and his face clean-shaven.

All heads turned as Sam's daughter, Nikki, started up the aisle in her red knee-length dress with white lace trim. She reached into her basket and pulled out rose petals that she tossed onto the aisle runner.

Emma was next. A big smile filled her face. Everyone was happy about this wedding. And then Hannah started up the aisle. Her steps were slow and measured as she held a small bouquet of ivory and red roses with holly berries and long-needle pine.

The music changed to the wedding march. The crowd stood. And the bride started up the aisle. Helen beamed with happiness. It wasn't her stunning ivory gown or her lush bouquet that caught and held people's attention. It was the glowing smile that she bestowed upon her groom as she made her way toward him. She looked at him like he was the only person in the church.

Darla expelled a dreamy sigh. That was the way all weddings should be. A bride and groom should look at each other like they were the only two in the entire room. Their love was palpable and filled the church with an undeniable warmth.

When Darla faced forward, her gaze automatically landed on Will. She could imagine it being that way if she were to walk down the aisle to Will just as they had planned all those years ago. If only there was a way to undo the past.

Just then Will's gaze moved over the crowd. It stopped and lingered on her. Her heart tap-tapped. Maybe, just maybe, this wasn't the end. Maybe it was just the beginning.

20

I dos were exchanged.

The pronouncement of husband and wife was made.

And a kiss was shared.

Will was so happy for his father. He'd followed them down the aisle and out the door. The sleigh was waiting for them. Spotlights had been set up near the walk to highlight the sleigh and the horses with their holiday jingle bells. Everyone rushed outside to watch the happy couple make their grand exit.

When Helen's gaze landed on the sleigh, she gasped. It took her a moment to find her voice. Then she turned to her groom. "Is this what you were keeping from me?"

His father smiled and nodded. "I wanted to surprise you."

"You did." She turned her attention back to the horse and sleigh before returning it to his father. There were happy tears sparkling in her eyes. "You most definitely did. Thank you."

"I'd like to take the credit, but it was Will and Darla

who made my idea a reality."

Helen rushed over to Will and hugged him. "Thank you so much."

"I can't take all of the credit. Darla did a lot of it."

And then she glanced around for Darla, who appeared to be lost in the crowd. "Will you make sure to thank her for me?"

"I will"

As Helen returned to the groom's side and rewarded him with a kiss, Will couldn't deny a sense of contentment at a job well done.

The guests surged forward on the freshly shoveled sidewalks as the newlyweds climbed into the sleigh. A heavy white blanket awaited them to keep them snug on their ride. The photographer snapped a dozen or so photos of them from all angles. And then Darla's father had agreed to guide the sleigh through town. They were off to ride through the streets of Bluestar before ending up at their destination—the reception.

Will turned around, hoping to find Darla, but there were so many wedding guests he couldn't find her. He couldn't linger as he had to get to the community center because they were having a reception line there, and he was expected to be a part of it.

He gave the departing crowd one more scan but still couldn't locate Darla. He knew she'd been at the wedding because he'd spotted her seated in the church. And when their gazes had caught, he'd felt his heart pound in his chest. It just confirmed what everyone had been telling him—to tell Darla everything and let her decide what she wanted. Because he knew what he wanted—her.

He climbed into his father's cart and waited to get in the long line to the community center. The only time there was a traffic jam in Bluestar was when there was a wedding or funeral. Thankfully, today it was the former. He couldn't help but smile, as in front of him there was a solid line of carts, and behind him all he could see were the headlights of more carts.

It took some time to make his way to the community center, but he'd finally arrived and found a parking spot right in front. The space had been reserved for the bride and groom, as this was their getaway vehicle. Hannah and Emma already had plans to decorate it with a "Just Married" sign and streamers.

Once inside, the receiving line was formed, and the guests streamed through one by one. Hands were shaken, hugs were given, and best wishes abounded. He was pretty certain that Helen and his father had permanent smiles pinned to their faces. They definitely made a great couple.

And then Darla stood before him. The breath caught in his lungs. She sent him a smile that rose up and made her eyes sparkle like gems. His heart leapt with joy. He was so worried she was going to hate him for the rest of his life. And then he expelled the breath he hadn't realized he'd been holding.

He sent her a tentative smile as his heart *thump-thumped* in his chest. His gaze took in her deep blue dress, which hugged her curves in the most flattering way. "You look beautiful."

"Thank you." Her cheeks filled with color. "You look really good too."

"Oh, this old thing," he said jokingly. "I pulled it out of the back of my closet."

"Well, it looks really good on you."

"Thanks." And then it was time to speak up. "Could we talk later?"

She nodded. "I'd like that."

And then she moved on down the line. As he shook Aster's hand, his thoughts were still on his exchange with Darla. He recalled her smile. Did this mean she was no longer angry with him for keeping his cancer diagnosis from her? He could only hope so.

He didn't have long to think about it, as there were wedding photos to take, dinner to be served, and the best man speech to make. But throughout the evening, his gaze would scan the guests, searching for Darla. He didn't want her to disappear before they had a chance to speak.

The wedding was beautiful.

And the best man was so handsome in his suit and tie.

Throughout the evening, Darla found herself utterly distracted by Will. As the dinner dishes were being cleared from the table, she glanced down and realized she'd barely eaten a bite. It wasn't that the food wasn't good; it was all delicious. But her stomach was filled with what felt like a swarm of butterflies.

She had no idea what Will wanted to speak to her about. Was he going to say goodbye to her? Or was it

possible he wanted to try to patch things up between them? She fervently hoped it was the latter.

But with him being busy with his best man duties, there simply wasn't any time for them to have a moment alone. And so, she waited and made light conversation with Birdie and the other people at her table.

Emma stopped by their table. "Darla, would you mind doing me a big favor?"

"Sure. Whatever you need." She was more than happy to help.

"The wedding party is about to dance, and I was wondering if you would mind dancing with Will for me."

Darla was confused. "But I'm not part of the wedding party."

"It's fine. Aster is dancing with Sam. And Hannah is dancing with Ethan. I wouldn't ask, but I promised Nikki that we would do a little decorating." She held up a "Just Married" sign. "Please."

Nikki came running up to her aunt. "We have to hurry."

Darla smiled at the little girl's excitement. "I'd be happy to help out."

"Thank you." Emma smiled. "I already explained things to Will." She glanced over her shoulder. "And here he comes."

Darla followed her gaze to see Will headed in her direction. Emma and Nikki departed.

Will stopped next to Darla's chair and held his hand out to her. "May I have this dance?"

She placed her hand in his, immediately feeling a zing of excitement race up her arm and set her heart a flutter. "Yes, you may."

He led her to the edge of the dance floor. The bride and groom just finished their first dance as husband and wife. And then the wedding party and their escorts were asked to join them on the dance floor. Even after all of this time, it felt so natural to step into Will's arms.

Darla's feet didn't even feel as though they touched the floor as they moved around the dance floor. And her heart was beating so loud it echoed in her ears.

"It was a nice wedding," Will said, breaking the silence.

"It was absolutely lovely. Helen and Walter look so happy. And Nikki was so excited to go decorate the bride and groom's getaway vehicle."

"Oh, yes. That has been the topic of a lot of whispered conversations so the bride and groom don't catch on."

Darla smiled. "They are so happy. I wonder if they'll see anything tonight but each other."

They both glanced over at the bride and groom as they slowly swayed back and forth in the middle of the dance floor. They didn't seem to notice they weren't moving to the beat of the music. In fact, they didn't seem to notice that there was a large room full of people staring at them.

Darla wanted that sort of happiness. She wanted that love with Will. Because if she'd learned anything through all of this time apart, it was that they had something special—something she'd never been able to duplicate with anyone else.

When the song changed, Darla knew this wasn't the time or place for this conversation, but she felt they'd already waited much too long. And she just couldn't wait any longer.

"Will, there's something I need to say."

"There's something I need to say too." He glanced around as more couples joined the dance floor. "But not here. Come on."

He led her to the coat room. He handed over her coat, and she shrugged it on. It was quite possible with her heart beating so fast and the warmth emanating from her chest that she'd never notice the chill in the air.

Once outside, silence surrounded them except for the occasional laugh from Emma and Nikki in the distance as they decorated the newlywed's vehicle.

"Darla—"

"No. Let me speak first. I'm sorry I didn't take your news the other day better. At first, I was shocked. But that wasn't all of it. I've been so mad at you for so long for ruining our wedding. I was so busy being mad at you and wallowing in my hurt that I didn't realize that maybe you were right to have called things off."

"You think I was right? You didn't want to marry me?" Pain reflected in his eyes.

"Yes. I mean no." She took a calming breath. "I've been doing some thinking. And the problems between us started before your diagnosis. I planned a wedding that was far too big and expensive. But I was too proud or too stubborn to admit my mistake. And as the bills mounted,

I wasn't able to fly home to see my family. The longer I was away from them, the more homesick I became. But I couldn't admit any of that to you because I didn't want you to think less of me. So, the quieter I became the more distance loomed between us. No wonder you didn't want to tell me about the cancer."

"I wish I had known. I was so wrapped up in my job that I lost sight of everything else. I'm sorry. I would have helped you figure things out if I'd known. I just felt this looming distance between us."

"I'm sorry I didn't speak up. I promise it won't happen again. That is if you want to give us another chance." Her heart launched into her throat as she waited for his next words.

He took her hands into his own. "I'd like nothing more, but you have to understand my cancer came back once already. It could come back again. I would understand if that is a risk you aren't willing to take."

"Or it might not come back." She stared deeply into his eyes. "Either way, I want to be by your side because I think together we can accomplish anything."

He reached out and cupped her cheek. "I never stopped loving you."

"I never stopped loving you either—even when I was mad at you for dumping me."

"Trust me. I'll never made that mistake again. Life without you just isn't the same."

He leaned toward her as she lifted up on her tiptoes. His lips pressed to hers, sending a cascade of goosebumps trailing down her skin. If this was a dream, she never wanted to wake up. Because after so long, she finally felt as though she was truly at home.

The sound of the door opening drew them apart. They stepped out of the way to let a couple of guests pass. Darla's purse slipped from her shoulder. As she caught it, she recalled the gift in it. She unsnapped the catch and pulled out the red shimmery paper-wrapped package with a white satin ribbon.

She held it out to Will. "I have a Christmas present for you."

His gaze moved from hers to the gift and back again. "But I don't have one for you."

"You already gave me the best Christmas present ever—your love." She placed the gift in his hand. "Go ahead. Open it."

"Shouldn't I save it for Christmas?"

"I can't wait that long."

"Darling, Christmas is tomorrow."

She smiled at his use of her pet name. "I can't wait until tomorrow. Go ahead. Open it."

He slid off the white ribbon and then tore off the paper to find a little white box. He lifted the top and then withdrew a keychain with blue sea glass with a tiny heart cutout.

As the keychain dangled from his finger, he said, "It reminds me of when we were in school and we'd go walking on the beach where we'd collect sea glass. Life was so easy back then."

"I was hoping it would remind you of those times. And now you will always have my heart with you wherever you go." She smiled at him.

"Thank you. I'll never be without it." And then he pointed upward.

She lifted her head and found they were standing under the mistletoe. When her gaze lowered, Will was staring at her with love reflecting in his eyes. He pulled her close. And then their lips pressed together.

This was the best Christmas ever.

EPILOGUE

Valentine's Day
Bluestar Island

A romantic evening lay ahead.

It was all Will would tell her.

Darla was so excited. Each time they were separated, she missed him terribly. Video chatting and phone calls just weren't the same thing as being in the same room with him. And she had some really exciting news to share with him.

She'd just finished her shift at the café and was headed to her apartment. It was already dark out. She couldn't wait until summer arrived and the days were longer.

She checked the time. It was five o'clock. Will had been cryptic during their last phone conversation. But he'd told her to be ready at five forty-five. Only then would she learn the details of their evening.

They had so much to celebrate tonight, from their renewed love to her signing not only with a literary agent but this morning she'd signed her first book contract. It felt as though at last all of the pieces of her life were falling into place.

She slipped her key into the doorknob and opened the door. Inside, she found the room illuminated with candles. She gasped. *What is going on?*

Her gaze scanned the room. There was a note on the counter:

Not much longer and we'll be together.
See you very soon,
Will

She smiled as she rushed off to the bathroom to shower. She wanted to look her best for Will.

At exactly five forty-four, she emerged from her bedroom in her little black dress with black heels. She was so excited to see Will it didn't matter to her if they ate in or out. She also knew without a reservation, they wouldn't be able to get a table in Bluestar. Tonight, was the busiest night for dining out of the entire year.

Anticipation thrummed through her veins. Since Christmas Eve, they'd started talking about everything and they hadn't stopped. They'd discussed the present as well as the future—their future. The plans included making San Francisco their primary residence, but they'd maintain the house on Bluestar for their many visits.

But there was one thing Will wouldn't talk to her about—this evening's plans…

Knock-knock.

Her heart fluttered in her chest. A smile pulled at the

corners of her lips. She rushed to the door and flung it open, eager to throw herself into Will's arms. But Will wasn't standing there. In fact, no one was on the other side of the doorway.

What in the world? She peered around but there was no sign of anyone. She was just about to close the door when she saw a red envelope sitting on the ground. When she bent over to pick it up, she saw her name scrolled in black ink. She quickly opened it.

You are the light of my life.
Follow the lit path to find your surprise.

I love you,
Will

Her heart *pitter-pattered* in her chest as her smile grew. What was he up to? She didn't wait around to figure it out. Thankfully, the snow had melted and she could wear her heels. With her red dress coat and white knit scarf, she was ready for her surprise evening. She had no idea what he was up to, but even if it was a walk through Beachcomber Park, she would be happy. Just being with Will filled her heart to overflowing.

When she opened the door again, she noticed battery-operated candles flickering. They were lined on either side of the walkway. She followed them out to the sidewalk, and there waiting for her was the sleigh with a driver and two beautiful white horses.

This was for her? Her heart swooned. The sleigh was

decorated with white and red twinkle lights. Darla's eyes filled with happy tears. She blinked repeatedly, not wanting to ruin her carefully done makeup.

She was helped inside and a heavy blanket covered her lap. Thanks to Will getting the sleigh's wheels working again, it could be used with or without snow. She couldn't help but wonder where Will was waiting for her.

With her snug beneath the blanket, they passed through town. More candles lit the way. He must have bought out an entire candle company. There went her waterworks again. She dabbed at her eyes.

The people of Bluestar, her friends, guests at the café, and even her parents were standing along the sidewalk. They waved and sent her best wishes. It was like they were all in on this surprise.

Darla couldn't blame everyone for being curious. After years of being proclaimed the perfect couple, they'd let things fall apart. Then again, maybe they were supposed to put a pause on their relationship. Because if they'd never been apart—given a chance to figure out life on their own—how were they ever supposed to appreciate having someone in their life through the good and the bad.

Before their breakup, she'd come to take Will for granted. She'd just assumed he would always be there, loving her and she loving him. But that wasn't the case. Relationships took time and effort—even after saying I do. That was the lesson she'd learned. It was one she hoped to never forget.

When the sleigh pulled to a stop, it was in front of

A LIGHTHOUSE CAFÉ CHRISTMAS

the Pizza Pie Shoppe. This was the place where they'd had their first date. Her heart *pitter-pattered* faster.

The driver helped her out of the sleigh. Another path of candles led her to the front door. A server opened it for her. And when she stepped inside, a hush fell over the room. Her gaze swept over the crowded room until it came to rest on Will, who was sitting at "their" table in the far corner.

She headed straight for him. He stood. When she reached him, she immediately wrapped her arms around him. "No one has ever done something so sweet for me."

He pulled back and gazed into her eyes. "Happy Valentine's. We missed a lot of holidays together, and I plan to do my best to make our future ones extra special."

"You've outdone yourself. Thank you."

"It's not over yet."

"It's not? I can't imagine what you've missed." She couldn't stop smiling. She was so happy.

He pulled something out of his pocket and the next thing she knew, he was down on one knee. "Darla, I was a fool to let you go once. I never plan to make that mistake again. You are my best friend and the bright shining star in my life. I love you with all of my heart." Then he opened a black velvet box and held it out to her. "Will you marry me?"

This time there was no holding back the tears of joy. They spilled onto her cheeks and she nodded. "I will. I love you too."

He pulled a large diamond ring from the box and

slipped it onto her finger. The oval diamond was surrounded with smaller stones and sparkled in the light. It was a new ring. A new ring for a new start.

It was only then that Darla noticed everyone around them cheering. She held up her hand to give them a glimpse of the ring.

Then she leaned into Will. "How did you manage all of this?"

"I had a little help. Actually, it was a lot of help from your friends and family. They wanted you to have your happily-ever-after."

Darla was deeply touched. More happy tears flowed. The town had once more pulled together, and this time they'd succeeded in creating the most special night of her life. She didn't know how she'd ever thank them, but she'd think of that tomorrow. Tonight, she had other things to occupy her.

She gazed into her fiancé's eyes. "All I'll ever need is you in my life."

He wrapped his arms around her. "You have me forever."

She lifted onto her tiptoes and pressed her lips to his. No matter where they lived or what they did, she would be home as long as she was with Will.

Want to read more about Darla and Will's happily-ever-after? Sign up for my newsletter and receive a Bonus Epilogue where these two say, "I do." You can sign up for my newsletter at https://www.jenniferfaye.com/newsletter/

Darla's Frosted Sugar Cookies

INGREDIENTS

Cookies:
8 oz Cream Cheese, softened
¾ cup unsalted butter, softened
1 cup sugar
3 tsp vanilla
2 ¼ cups flour
½ tsp baking soda

Frosting:
2 cups powdered sugar
7-8 tsp whole milk
4 tsp light corn syrup
½ tsp vanilla extract
food coloring

Cookies:
- Preheat oven to 350°F
- Beat cream cheese, butter, sugar and vanilla until well blended.
- Add baking soda. Blend. Slowly add flour, blending after each small addition until all flour is blended.
- Refrigerate for an hour minimum.
- Roll and cut into your favorite shapes. And decorate.

- Bake 10 to 12 minutes.

Frosting:
- Combine first four ingredients. Stir until frosting is smooth. Add more milk until spreadable consistency.
- Divide frosting into separate bowls for each desired color. Add food coloring drop by drop until desired shade.
- Decorate cookies and enjoy.

Thanks so much for reading Darla and Will's story. I hope their journey made your heart smile. If you did enjoy the book, please consider...

- Help spreading the word about A Lighthouse Café Christmas by writing a review.

- [Subscribe to my newsletter](#) in order to receive information about my next release as well as find out about giveaways and special sales.

- You can like my author page on [Facebook](#) or follow me on [Twitter](#).

I hope you'll come back to Bluestar Island and read the continuing adventures of its residents. In upcoming books, there will be updates on Darla and Will as well as the addition of some new islanders.

Coming next will be Emma's story!

Thanks again for your support! It is **HUGELY** appreciated.

Happy reading,

Jennifer

Other titles available by Jennifer Faye include:

WHISTLE STOP ROMANCE SERIES:
A Moment to Love
A Moment to Dance
A Moment on the Lips
A Moment to Cherish
A Moment at Christmas

WEDDING BELLS IN LAKE COMO:
Bound by a Ring & a Secret
Falling for Her Convenient Groom

ONCE UPON A FAIRYTALE:
Beauty & Her Boss
Miss White & the Seventh Heir
Fairytale Christmas with the Millionaire

THE BARTOLINI LEGACY:
The Prince and the Wedding Planner
The CEO, the Puppy & Me
The Italian's Unexpected Heir

GREEK ISLAND BRIDES:
Carrying the Greek Tycoon's Baby
Claiming the Drakos Heir
Wearing the Greek Millionaire's Ring

Click here to find all of Jennifer's titles and buy links.

About the Author

Award-winning author, Jennifer Faye pens fun, heartwarming contemporary romances with rugged cowboys, sexy billionaires and enchanting royalty. With more than a million books sold, she is internationally published with books translated into more than a dozen languages. She is a two-time winner of the RT Book Reviews Reviewers' Choice Award, the CataRomance Reviewers' Choice Award, named a TOP PICK author, and been nominated for numerous other awards.

Now living her dream, she resides with her very patient husband and two spoiled cats. When she's not plotting out her next romance, you can find her curled up with a mug of tea and a book. You can learn more about Jennifer at www.JenniferFaye.com

Subscribe to Jennifer's periodic newsletter for news about upcoming releases and other special offers.

You can also join her on Twitter, Facebook, or Goodreads.

Made in the USA
Monee, IL
10 November 2021